CALLUM
McBRIDE

CALLUM McBRIDE

MICHAEL RIDING

Matador
9 Priory Business Park,
Wistow Road, Kibworth Beauchamp,
Leicestershire. LE8 0RX
Tel: 0116 279 2299
Email: books@troubador.co.uk
Web: www.troubador.co.uk/matador
Twitter: @matadorbooks

ISBN 978 1838593 254

British Library Cataloguing in Publication Data.
A catalogue record for this book is available from the British Library.

Printed and bound in the UK by TJ International, Padstow, Cornwall
Typeset in 11pt Gill Sans by Troubador Publishing Ltd, Leicester, UK

Matador is an imprint of Troubador Publishing Ltd

To: Oliver, Sam, John, Lucy,
and happy memories on Mull.

Contents

FROM THE AUTHOR

Callum McBride was written for a young person who found it really hard to put down their electronics and read a book. I hope that you enjoy it. If you can't put your electronics down for long then you can visit *www.callummcbride.co.uk* and go to the gallery and see some of the places and the animals that feature in the book.

I would also love to hear from you. Tell me if you liked the book or if you didn't, and tell me what would have made it better.

You can contact me at *author@callummcbride.com* or via Twitter *@MichaelRiding18* or via Facebook *www.facebook.com/michael.riding.127* or via Instagram on *michaelridingauthor*

Michael Riding

CHAPTER 1

MONDAY MORNING

It was the same dream again.

It made him uneasy, although he supposed that all dreams could do that. It made him feel as if he wasn't quite himself. He'd had the dream several times over the last few months. It would begin with a feeling of disorientation and nausea; then when he awoke, he felt cold and sweaty, and with a feeling of wretchedness in the pit of his stomach. Even in his dream it reminded him of the feeling he got when he had done something stupid and was sent to the headteacher of his school, just worse, much much worse.

In his dream, he was swimming in the Sound of Iona, between the Isle of Mull off the north west coast of Scotland and the small deeply spiritual island of Iona. This was the same sacred place where St. Columba first landed

1

from Ireland and set up his monastery, bringing Christianity to the Scots. It was early in the evening, and the waves were small and choppy, kicked up by the south-westerly wind that was blowing in from the North Atlantic. His head was sticking out of the clear emerald green water and was looking up at the ferry. It was very close, but his eyes were blurred. There was some kind of a struggle on the deck, and he could hear what he thought was a scream. It was muted, and he doubted if anyone else had heard it because of the surrounding noise of the wind. In what seemed like just a moment from when he first heard the scream, came a loud splash. He dived underwater and swam towards the splash. His vision was better under the water and he could hear everything clearly.

He reached the source of the splash very quickly, far quicker than he could have thought possible, only to find that it was a young woman. She was pretty, with long blonde hair that fanned out in the water like that of a mermaid; although she looked as if she had been ill for a long time. It was clear that he was too late, that she was already dead; he could sense the death, although he didn't quite know how. It was a recent death, and that would mean that the flesh was good. He swam forward, gliding through the water with a grace and effortlessness that he had never before experienced. He nudged the body just a little, and it turned over in the water. Those long locks of blonde hair were suspended in a halo around features that he imagined would have been striking in life, but in death, were just empty. Part of him felt sad, and part of him just felt hungry. He nudged the body again and opened his massive jaws.

Callum awoke in that same cold state of sweatiness. The dream slowly slipped away as he regained his awareness. As always, it was the pretty face of the young woman that faded last, but even as he closed his eyes and tried to hold it in his mind, it gradually faded and slipped out of his grasp, as it always did. The last sensation Callum had that was connected with the dream was sadness. He knew that at his age, all sorts of strange things could happen. His voice had been wobbling recently, and in his final lesson of the school year he had tried to answer a question, and all that came out was a squeaky croak. His supposed 'best' friend, Andrew Nair, had led the laughter and the humiliation. Callum sighed and instantly forgave his friend as he had done the same himself on many occasions. Lying in his bed, he reflected that maybe everyone sometimes did things that they weren't particularly proud of. He decided that the next time he realised he was doing something that he would later be ashamed of, he would definitely not do it … or at least try not to do it anyway.

He supposed that all soon-to-be teenagers had funny dreams and began to calm down. He remembered that it was the 26th of June and therefore the first day of the long summer holiday, and he was at home in his own bed. His own bed was in the loft room of the ferryman's cottage in Fionnphort (Fin-a-fort) on Mull, where he lived with his mum and dad and on occasion, his elder brother and sister. It was only up until a few years ago that he shared this room with his brother Iain. The cottage was built in a traditional Scottish style with white walls and a black slate roof. The house was a one and a half storey, which meant

3

he had dormer windows in his bedroom in the roof space. His bedroom window looked straight out over the sandy beach and across the half a mile stretch that was the Sound of Iona. Sometimes, Callum liked to sit in his window in the teeth of a gale looking straight into the fury of the Atlantic storms, at least until Mr or Mrs McBride came up and made him close the window.

He looked at his watch and saw that it was already 8 am and that if he didn't hurry he would be late for his breakfast. He stopped for just a little longer and peered out of his window, gazing across the sound towards the abbey on Iona.

The Abbey was being restored after many years of neglect. Iona had been one of the greatest Christian centres ever since Columba had landed there from Ireland in 563 AD and was later made a saint. Callum wasn't a particularly religious person, but he had to admit that there was something spiritual about the beautiful island of Iona. As always it was amazing to him that he could look out of his bedroom window and see a different sight every morning. Yes, the quay was always there where the ferry came and went, and where the sightseeing boats went to and from the island of Staffa; as was the hill and the beaches, the church and the motley collection of small boats, but, it was the light that changed. Every time he looked, and he had looked thousands of times, the scene was subtly different.

"Cal! Will you get yoursen dressed and doon the stairs!" It was his mum, Mrs McBride calling.

Mrs McBride was a district nurse for the local community, and the fiercest person Callum had ever met.

4

She was short with deep-red hair and was nearly as wide as she was tall. She spoke with a strong Scottish brogue and Callum had yet to meet the person who would argue with her. Although Callum now stood a good 10 cm taller than her, he had only ever dared to answer her back once. It was not something he was inclined to do ever again. Her retribution was fearsome and swift. In fact, Callum didn't like to think about it at all, but when he did, his hand automatically recalled that day and immediately went to his right bottom cheek. How embarrassing was it to have been put over her knee and spanked like that? Spanked like a 3 year old in the middle of the local shop! Still, the people in the shop didn't laugh, and no one spoke of it then, and no one spoke of it afterwards. Not because they didn't think it was funny; Callum was absolutely sure that they did think it was funny, Callum was sure that those that had witnessed the spectacle and those that had subsequently been told of it in whispers, thought that it was hilarious. No, the reason nobody spoke about it to him directly, was that they were afraid he would tell Mrs McBride and that she might well do it to them.

None of his teachers at Oban High School came even close to being so scary, and all of Callum's friends were scared to death of Mrs McBride; even though half of them had been brought into the world by her.

Mrs McBride could put the fear of the Devil into Callum when she had a mind to, and it wasn't that her bark was worse than her bite, it was just that he knew that she was a good-hearted person. After all, it had been her who had persuaded Mr McBride to adopt Callum after he had been found on a seat in the lounge on the 'Loch Speive' (the ferry from Iona to Mull).

Callum had been found at the beginning of summer on the last ferry back to Fionnphort from Iona on a Saturday. He had been found by one of the crew, Seamus Dougherty, who had gone to investigate a small package that appeared to be wriggling. Not only was this strange package wriggling, but it smelled bad too. Not wanting to get involved in anything that wriggled and smelled bad, Seamus had gone to tell his Captain. It just so happened to be Mr McBride who was working that shift. His Captain was a taciturn man, a man of few words, all of which were considered carefully. Captain McBride was not a bit like his wife, although he too commanded respect. He was 6 feet 2 inches tall and had a black beard peppered with flecks of grey that made the few words that he spoke difficult to understand. He spoke in a deep gruff voice that sounded like the noise that big pebbles on a beach make when the waves drag them over each other; or the noise that thunder in the next valley makes.

When Captain McBride saw the package he grunted, "Och, it's nobut a wee bairn, gi'it to the wife an she'll hav it sorted". So that is exactly what happened. Callum, all wrapped up in his blankets was given to Mrs McBride, and he was sorted. Of course, they called the police, but it was a Saturday night and nothing could be done until Monday when social services got back to work in Oban on the mainland. After all, Mrs McBride was the district nurse, so who better to look after an abandoned baby?

Monday arrived, and social services came out to see the situation. The baby looked fit and well so the decision was made to leave him where he was until the mother could be found. The police searched Iona and put up posters, there was even a TV appeal, and Callum's picture was broadcast to more than 50 million homes, but no one had lost a baby.

After a few months, people had got bored with the baby that had been found on the ferry. He had been nicknamed by Iain the McBride's oldest son, then 14, as 'Cal'. This was short for Calmac, the name of the ferry company and in time it got lengthened to Callum. Nearly a year after he was found, Mrs McBride, in a rare moment of intimacy, turned to Captain McBride and whispered, "Shall we keep the wee one then?"

"Aye," was the gravelly response, and Callum had a mum and dad. The adoption papers went through, and Callum was christened in the local church as 'Callum McBride.'

"Callllllllllluuuuuuuuum!"

Callum shook himself out of his reverie and made his way to the family bathroom to brush his hair and teeth. He caught a quick look at himself in the mirror. He was a good-looking lad if he didn't mind admitting it to himself. His family were all dark with hints of ginger, but he was fair and blonde, tall for his age with big blue eyes and eyelashes that most women would sell their souls for. He was quite an athlete and had done well at the end of term sports day…one of his happier memories from school.

He went downstairs to breakfast and marvelled at the delicious smell that greeted him; smoked mackerel, caught by Iain who was back from his job in Glasgow. Iain, a CID policeman, was now 27. This visit home, he had brought a girlfriend, Lauren, back with him for a week's stay. Despite Iain returning to Glasgow the previous afternoon, the legacy of his smoked mackerel remained for Callum to enjoy. Iain and Callum had crossed when Callum returned home from his final week's boarding before the end of term. Iain had been 14 when Callum was adopted, and they weren't close, although Iain always had a kindly word. "How's it going Boat Boy?" (Iain's latest nickname for Callum), he had said as he ruffled Callum's hair. "I reckon you are old enough to borrow my boat, but trash it and you die!" had been his parting words.

This was a gift from his elder brother that Callum couldn't help but grin at…a foolish grin like a 4 year old at Christmas or a lad at the cinema on his first date. Iain's small skiff represented freedom; freedom to roam the island from the sea, freedom to go fishing, freedom to visit Iona, and freedom to be on his own on the sea that he loved.

With that happy thought in mind, he went out of the house and down on to the beach for a walk in the beautiful July sunshine. He had nothing whatsoever to do, and although he knew he would get bored within the hour, until then he was determined to enjoy; no homework, no chores, no responsibilities, nothing!

Today was going to be a long and beautiful summer's day and Callum was determined to enjoy it. As he wandered on the beach he could feel the heat from the sun on top of his head. It could certainly get hot in Fionnphort, but when it did it created a wonderful cooling onshore breeze, and although it was still early in the day he could feel the first stirrings on his face.

Callum crossed the beach and turned right, away from the village. This led in only a few metres to the granite hills that determined the colour and shape of the end of the Ross of Mull. Callum started to climb and after a few minutes he came to his favourite spot in the whole world. This was the top of the hill where he could see forever. Laid out in front of him was the whole of Iona. To the south is Fionnphort, to the west is the Sound of Iona, and behind him to the east, the foreboding mountains in the heart of Mull. Beyond Iona, Callum could see the islands of Tiree and Coll, to the north was the closer isle of Staffa with the tourist boats that carted sixty people at a time to marvel at the columnar basalt that once came pouring out of a fissure when the Atlantic Ocean was being made. Billions of tons of white-hot molten rock that spread out from Mull even as far as Northern Ireland. The basalt cooled and solidified leaving behind these amazing columns. Callum had been on one of the trips the previous year and had marvelled with the tourists, but now as he lay back under the azure blue sky he was daydreaming about taking his brother's boat out to Staffa.

As Callum lay back thinking of the potential that was caught up in his brother's boat, he felt a pang of anger. Callum didn't enjoy school. Along with all the other children in the area he was sent to boarding school in Oban, out to Oban on Sunday afternoon back Friday night. Every week, week in week out. Unfortunately, his nightmares had started to scare the other pupils in the dormitory, and he found over time, he had fewer and fewer friends.

He had been looking forward to spending time with his best friend Andrew who had moved to Fionnphort when he was five. His parents were both doctors from Yorkshire. They had come to the island after Andrew's little sister had died in a terrible accident, the sort of accident that no one believes will ever happen to them, but does occasionally happen to someone. She had been running through the kitchen in her socks at the age of three and had slipped. She had fallen awkwardly and had landed on her arm, which had broken. The broken end of the arm bone had entered her chest and all the skills of both her parents had not been enough to save her. She had died in the arms of her mother while Andrew and his dad looked on. Needless to say, this terrible tragedy had affected Andrew and his family badly. They felt that moving to Mull would give them the space they needed to heal, both giving up medicine when they moved.

Callum had adopted Andrew on his first day of primary school where they went in the local village of Bunessan. Andrew was scared to death; he spoke with a strange accent, he didn't understand half of what was said to him, and he didn't know a soul. When Callum went up to him in the playground and asked him if he would like to join in the other kids' games, he was awash with relief and gratitude. They had been firm friends ever since.

Andrew's parents then took the decision that if he was going to have to board anyway, he was to go to a public school in England. This meant that Andrew and Callum could only see each other in the holidays, and this holiday Andrew was going to the south of France for the first two weeks with a 'new' friend. It was this notion that was making Callum angry now as he had been looking forward to the same long summer like last year when they had roamed far and wide across the peat bogs, through the bog cotton, to beaches they had never seen before to find adventure in the great desolate outdoors that is Mull. Callum sighed to himself and felt the little knot of anger slip away…if the weather held and with Iain's boat he knew he could have a good time on his own.

Just as Callum was thinking this, as he was lying on his back with the sweet smell of the grass in his nose and the sound of a munching sheep in his ears, he spotted a buzzard above him and to the right. Buzzards are common in Mull and this one was obviously out hunting. Callum watched as the buzzard circled and then dropped thirty metres or so and circled again. Callum wondered what it would be like to be the buzzard. He imagined what it would be like to be flying above his prone body searching for prey, feeling the wind in his feathers…and then he was.

Callum felt a wave of nausea and disorientation… just like in his dreams, which passed quickly. At first, he felt confused. He couldn't place himself, he couldn't make sense of what he was seeing. His vision was clearer than he could ever have imagined. He was looking down on his own body and he could see all around him with incredible detail. He was circling very high up but he wasn't scared that he would fall because he could see his body lying where he had left it. WHERE HE HAD LEFT IT. What was he thinking? Where he had left it on top of the hill? How could he have left it on top of the hill? Callum felt confused and scared. What was happening to him? First the dreams and now this!

11

He was awake, how could he be flying around just where the buzzard had been?

Before Callum could even begin to make sense of what was happening he became aware that his vision had focussed on a small brown shape about a hundred metres from where his body lay. He felt his vision concentrate, it was almost like focussing on something through binoculars although the brown shape didn't get bigger. It just got incredibly clear. It was a rabbit; the buzzard was hunting a rabbit. Just as it dawned on him what was happening, the buzzard dived. It felt like time had slowed right down, and almost came to a complete standstill. Although he knew that the buzzard was diving at over a hundred miles an hour, it took an age to fall towards the rabbit. As the rabbit got closer and closer he could see it in perfect detail. It was a humbling experience to see out of eyes that were evolved to such a level of incredible clarity. The rabbit was sitting there, chewing the tender grass shoots that it had found in a small hollow near the summit of the hill. Blissfully unaware of its fate until a shadow fell across it; the rabbit sat frozen with fear. Even as Callum's senses took in the incredible dive, he was able to think that the buzzard was a juvenile; still learning its craft. A skilled adult would never have allowed its shadow to alert the rabbit to its presence. This time it looked as if the buzzard would be lucky. The rabbit was also young and was frozen to the spot with terror. Callum could see the fear in its eyes that were now approaching at a phenomenal speed. Even with the incredible speed of the dive, Callum was able to see the rabbit in minute detail. He could see the individual hairs on the rabbit's back, the whiskers standing on edge, and unbelievably, an insect crawling just behind one of the rabbit's ears. Callum felt sorry for the rabbit and for a brief moment he wondered what it would be like to be sat there frozen in terror, racked with indecision and not knowing what to do in order to survive; perhaps knowing that a premature death was only seconds away.

Again he was hit with a wave of disorientation and nausea, and again it took him a little while to realise what he was feeling and seeing. Terror flowed over him gripping his insides with an empty hollow feeling, he felt a wave of helplessness and hopelessness and he knew that he was going to die. His vision was much poorer than it had been only a few moments ago, but it was enough to see the buzzard just centimetres above him. Its wings were flared and its talons outstretched, certainty in its eyes. The certainty of the kill.

The talons struck with an unimaginable force, breaking his back instantly, he felt no pain from below his waist. These same talons sank deep into his neck, releasing a spasm of pain, the like of which he had never felt before. Then it was over, he felt the beak rip into his flesh, and he felt his life force ebbing away. He tried to cry out, he tried to scream. A scream that carried all the pain and injustice of life; of life, and of death.

"Are you alright?"

"Are you alright?"

It was a girl's voice. Perhaps it was the voice of an angel thought Callum. He could still feel the memory of the excruciating pain felt by the rabbit just before it died; its life force taken in a fraction of a second by the buzzard, just doing what it had to do to survive.

"Are you alright?"

Callum looked up to see a girl, she was about the same age as him. She looked a little wild in shorts and an old tatty tee-shirt that looked at least three sizes too big, with short brown hair. In fact it was only the voice until you looked closely, that suggested it was a girl at all.

"Aye, I'm OK," whispered Callum.

"You were crying," said the girl. She wasn't saying it like the kids at school might, in an accusatory tone. She was just stating a fact.

"I know…I had a bad dream," muttered Callum.

"What were you dreaming?" asked the girl, and without giving him a chance to reply she said, "My name is Emma, what's yours?"

Callum looked at Emma for a few seconds. She reminded him of a wren, he decided. A bit too perky for his liking, with her head on one side, waiting for him to answer.

"Callum," he said.

"I live in the new cottage behind the Columba Centre. I'm English. Do you live here or are you on holiday?"

"You ask a lot of questions," said Callum beginning to feel slightly annoyed.

"Yes, I do," said Emma.

There was an uncomfortable silence for a few seconds, although Callum got the feeling that it was only uncomfortable for him, as Emma stood looking down at him with her hands loosely held together in front of her. He stood up to realise that he was only a few centimetres taller than Emma. He also noticed that she was quite pretty with pale skin and enormous brown eyes. You could see all the way around her iris, which was shaded under long brown lashes.

These blinked at him as she said "Well?"

"Well, what?"

"I-live-in-the-cottage-behind-the-Columba-Centre. I'm-English. Do-you-live-here-or-are-you-on-holiday?"

Emma said this slowly as if she was talking to a very small child. Callum thought he must have been mistaken when he thought she was pretty because now he could tell that she wasn't pretty at all, she was just annoying.

"Goodbye," he said and started away back down the hill. Who did she think she was? Climbing to his favourite spot and then patronising him!

"Sorry!" He heard her shout behind his back, "I didn't mean to upset you!" He ignored her and carried on walking. When he was a hundred metres away, he risked a backwards glance, to see her sitting in his spot, on top of the hill with her arms around her knees. He had the distinct impression that she wasn't very happy.

Callum went home to make his lunch as both his mum and dad would be out at work. He wanted to talk to Andrew about what had happened on the top of the hill, and about the dreams he had been having. He supposed that it was a bit strange that the only person he wanted to talk to was a friend rather than family. He knew that Andrew wouldn't laugh. Andrew would listen and probably suggest something really sensible like "Callum, I think you'll find it was sunstroke or temporary insanity brought on by hormonal changes in a pubescent boy. It can happen you know, I've read about it in New Scientist!" It was a shame that his friend wasn't here, even if he was a bit of a science nerd.

He couldn't tell his mum or dad. They just weren't that sort of family. He imagined what the reply would be if he told his dad that he had been first a buzzard and then a rabbit.

"Mother! The bairn's lost his marbles! You'll 'a te make an appointment wi' the heed Doctor!"

His mother would give him an Ibuprofen and send him to bed, his brother would ruffle his hair, roll his eyes and ask him if he had been sniffing glue. His sister would just say "Get lost pea brain."

They were a pretty normal family, all things considered. He loved them all dearly, and he knew that they loved him, but who do you tell that you think you're a rabbit? Maybe he should go and talk to the doctor. The local doctor, who's surgery was at Bunessan when he wasn't taking it on the road to Fionnphort or Iona, had retired last year and although Callum hadn't yet met his replacement, he had heard that he was keen on alternative therapies like acupuncture or aromatherapy or that foot rubbing one... was it chiropody or reflexology? Callum wasn't certain. Still, he wasn't sure that there was an alternative therapy for people thinking that they can see out of a buzzard's eyes and feel the pain of its prey as it died.

As Callum was washing up after his staple tuna and mayo sandwich, he caught sight of a lone figure walking along the beach. He picked the binoculars off the hook on the wall by the sink (because you never know when a school of dolphins could swim past along the sound) and saw that it was the strange girl he had met earlier, Emma. He was stabbed with a pang of guilt. He hadn't meant to be rude, but he'd just been eaten by a buzzard! How could you expect to be full of friendliness when you had just heard your backbone being scrunched by a one-metre wingspan raptor? Should he go and be nice? He had nothing else to do today. The problem was that if he was nice to her then he might get saddled with her for the next fortnight.

"Och Cal, ye've got yoursen a wee friend! Invite her fer tea", he could imagine his mother's voice and the big smile on her face. As soon as that happened, his life would be not worth living. In a village as small as Fionnphort, everybody knew everything. When he went into the Crossing Shop, the looks would be palpable.

"Have ye' heard? Wee Cal has a girlfriend!"

"What? Cal?"

"Aye"

"Who?"

"That wee English girl, the one staying beyond"

"Is she the one that looks like a boy?"

"Aye, that's the one."

"Do you no think that girls should have long hair?"

"Aye, ye know I do. It's confusing enough these days as it is with all those gay people and vegetarians an all."

Callum shuddered. No way.

Having had his lunch, Callum prepared to go out on his brother's boat. It was a four metre wooden skiff which Iain had rescued and repaired just a few years earlier. It was equipped with a 9 horsepower, Yamaha self-lubricating 2

17

stroke outboard engine. Callum loved to open it up, watch the bow shoot up in the air, and crash into the waves with spray flying up and being thrown over his head by the wind. That's what he needed now, some time in the boat would give him a chance to clear his mind.

As he walked down to the quay carrying his petrol can, he saw Emma again. He studiously ignored her and breathed a sigh of relief as he managed to walk past, without catching her eye. He walked the length of the old granite pier that these days was only used by the fishing boats when they wanted to beach their boats for the duration of a tide in order to carry out essential repairs. At the end of the pier, he scrambled on to the rocks and undid the pulley system that enabled the fishermen to retrieve their small boats that were anchored in the bay at any state of the tide. The boats are moored to an anchor that is below the low tide mark, which ensures the boat is always floating. Two ropes then run from the boat to a spike on the shore. Callum undid the ropes, and by pulling on one of them, he could pull his boat into the shore. He jumped in and untied the boat. The ropes would still be there when he returned and he could get out onto dry land and return the boat to its mooring. He connected the petrol tank to the engine, checked that it had enough two-stroke engine oil and pushed off from the pier. He stood up, aware that a crowd of tourists were watching him, and primed the engine. He put the engine down into its drive position and pulled the starting handle. The engine coughed and then sputtered into life.

Callum started to reverse the boat out into clearer water, he moved the lever on the engine into the forward position and opened her up at the same time turning the tiller to swing the boat around in a cool move, meant in part, to impress the tourists. The bow swung round and lifted as the engine roared, Callum felt the thrill of power and control, then disaster struck as the engine sputtered and died. The bow dropped and Callum no longer had control. Rats! thought Callum. How embarrassing was that? With his face blushing and twenty tourists or so watching, he tried to re-start the engine. He tried and failed. He tried everything he could think of, he gave the engine some choke…nothing, he opened up the throttle to give it more fuel and again nothing. Every time he tried to start it he had to stand and pull sharply on the starter cord, the luxury of an electric start was lost on an engine as small as this one. While he was panicking the boat was drifting stern first onto the main slipway. If it hit with the engine down it could wreck the engine. If he pulled up the engine and it hit without the engine down, it would scratch the boat, and he would have to leap out and get soaked. He would also look like a real DORK. Why hadn't he let the engine warm-up on its mooring like he was supposed to? How many times had his brother told him?

Just then Callum realised quite how stupid he had been, this painful realisation hit him as he caught sight of the Iona ferry coming around the end of the quay. The same one that he had been found on 12 years ago, the anniversary of which would be next week and was celebrated by his family as his birthday. He was now between the ferry and the slipway. If the ferry had to try to stop to avoid hitting him it would mean disaster. Although they weren't supposed to be, the ferries were constantly under pressure to get across to Iona and back as soon as possible. Occasionally they flew around the end of the short jetty and Callum wasn't sure that it would be able to stop; they didn't expect to see a small boat dead in the water just where they docked the ferry. When his dad found out, he wouldn't sit down for a week, and worse still would be the embarrassment as everybody would know. Iain would stop him from using the boat and everyone at school…Oh, it just didn't bear thinking about.

Come on now Callum, THINK! What can be stopping the engine from firing?

Just then it dawned on him what the problem must be! He hadn't opened the breathe-hole on the petrol can, so as the engine used the fuel it created a vacuum in the petrol tank and no more petrol could get through. Callum stood up and lunged for the tank in the front of the boat. He opened the breathe-hole and heard the air rush into the tank, this would allow the fuel to get to the engine. All he had to do now was re-prime the engine and… He turned around to go back to the stern to restart the engine and his heart leapt into his mouth, the boat was surfing in on a small wave and was about to crash, stern first, engine down, onto the slipway just in front of the Ferry that was looming above him. This was a complete and utter disaster! He was never going to be able to get out of the boat quickly enough to save the engine, and even if he could he would delay the ferry with everyone watching! Callum had that sick feeling in his stomach. The sick feeling that everyone gets when they've done something stupid and they are about to get caught. The same sick feeling he got in his dreams.

Just as Callum, frozen with fear, was watching disaster ride in on a small wave, someone walked purposefully out of the crowd of tourists, down the slip and into the water. It was Emma, and she had caught the boat just before it crashed onto the slipway.

"I'd start it if I were you," she said. As she spoke the ferry's horn sounded above Callum and he jumped. Without speaking he started the engine and roared out of the way of the ferry and away from the slip. With his face burning, he headed straight out into the sound.

Chapter 2

Monday Afternoon

While Callum was hugely relieved by his narrow escape on the quay, he was cringingly aware that it was only because of Emma, and that he owed her a huge debt. He was still thinking about it when he heard the 'Bing Bong' that was the start of the safety announcement made in both English and Gaelic that signalled the imminent departure of the ferry. He looked back to see that the tourists had all embarked, leaving just the one lonely looking figure on the quayside.

Aaargh! I don't want to! He thought to himself even as he turned the boat around and sped back to the quay. As he approached and Emma saw him, she turned away and started to walk up the quay, back to the village.

"Emma! Wait!" Callum shouted after her. "I'm sorry, thank you for helping just then." He could see the hesitation in her walk as she continued up the hill. Well I tried, Callum thought and started to turn away, and then almost without thinking he blurted out "Would you like to come for a ride in the boat?" Now what was he doing? He didn't even like this Emma and he was inviting her for a ride in the boat. Maybe no one would see them, he reasoned, if he was going to spend time with her, perhaps out at sea was the best place!

As soon as she heard the question he could see her shoulders lift. She turned around and asked, "Are you sure you know how to drive it?"

"Don't then," he replied and turned to go.

"No, I would love to come thank you. I don't mean to be rude you know. I didn't mean to say that you didn't know how to drive it. You looked like you knew what you were doing with it." Emma gabbled.

"I didn't earlier and ye saved me then," smiled Callum.

The deal done, it took only a few minutes to get a second lifejacket, for Emma to change her clothes that had got wet, and to grab some sweets from the shop. Then the pair of them roared out of the harbour heading across the sound to Iona.

"What are ye doin' up here?" he asked over the sound of the engine.

"My parents have bought a house here, they think it will be good for me to get away from London. I get asthma you know. They think that the air up here will clear my lungs. I also got into trouble at school and was asked to leave."

"What did you do?" asked Callum both secretly impressed and a little scared. He was out on his brother's

23

boat with a girl he'd never met before! She could be some psycho killer for all he knew.

"Told the truth."

"What do you mean?" asked Callum, now a little confused.

"I always tell the truth and I always say what I mean. That's why I upset people." Emma looked a little sad as she said this and started to look out of the front of the boat.

"What is that island called?" she asked Callum, pointing to the small island to the north of Iona.

"That's called Eilean Annraidh," Callum replied.

"Can we land there?" Emma asked.

"Aye, we can."

So they landed on the beach pulling the boat up a little way and finally sitting on top of the island.

"Callum?"

"Yes,"

"Why were you crying this morning?" Emma asked.

"Ye wouldn't believe me if I told you," Callum grunted, lying back on the grass watching the gulls flying overhead.

"You could always try me," said Emma.

Perhaps it was because he needed to tell someone. Perhaps it was because of the slightly strange way that she talked, without judgement in her voice. Perhaps it was because he thought that she wouldn't believe him anyway. Perhaps it was because she had such big brown eyes.

Whatever the reason, he did tell her. He told her all about the dreams and about what had happened earlier that morning. He told her about his family and about his friend Andrew. He told her about how he had become more and more unhappy at school. The whole time he had been talking Emma had listened. She didn't interrupt once. She didn't laugh, she didn't even move. Emma just listened. As his story came to an end, he began to realise quite how ridiculous the whole thing sounded, he slowed down and his words ground to a halt. He rolled away so as not to see Emma laugh at him, what was he thinking of? Bleating on like a deranged sheep with the most ridiculous story he'd ever heard!

Callum just lay on the grass. He could feel Emma's eyes on him. He was squirming inside with the embarrassment of it all. She wouldn't believe it. He wouldn't have believed her if their positions had been reversed. He would have laughed, told her she was stupid and then e-mailed Andrew to tell him about the crazy girl with ridiculous fantasies he'd met. Everyone in Fionnphort was used to slightly mad English people moving in, but this would be the best one ever! Minutes passed and he was feeling worse and worse, any second now she would tell him what a wally he was and laugh at him. She'd tell the whole village and he'd have to leave. Perhaps he could live with Iain for a while?

"I'll take you home," he grunted

"Wait," Emma said sounding thoughtful. "Can you do it when you want to?"

"Do what?"

"This teletransference thing?"

"This what?" he asked.

"Teletransference. Telekinetics is when you can move things with your mind, telepathy is when you can read minds and communicate with pure thought and teleportation is when you can move yourself with your mind. Teletransference is when you can transfer your mind into another. Normally it is a human into the mind of an animal as part of a drug-induced, religious ceremony."

"What do you mean it is 'normally'?" asked Callum incredulously. "Does this mean you believe me?"

"I'm not entirely sure yet," said Emma, "it is a bit far-fetched, but it has been reported before. Granted, it's usually reported by people who have taken drugs and most researchers put it down to hallucinations, but some of the reports give details that you wouldn't expect in hallucinations. There are some who believe it is possible."

"There are also some who believe in little green men, and ghosts, tooth fairies and Father Christmas!" said Callum vehemently.

"What? Don't you believe in Father Christmas?" asked Emma with her big brown eyes open even wider than normal. Then she laughed and so did Callum. The laughter sounded good to him and he realised that he hadn't laughed for quite a long time.

"Seriously though," said Callum after the laughter died away. "Do you believe me?"

"I want you to try something for me," replied Emma. "Try doing what you did this morning and see if you can get into the head of one of the gulls."

"Seagulls," said Callum.

"Gulls, there is no such thing as a seagull. There are only different sorts of gulls" answered Emma.

"Pedant!" accused Callum.

"I like things to be right," said Emma "now concentrate and see if you can be a 'gull'."

Callum tried to re-create in his mind what he had been thinking about earlier that morning when he had felt queasy and had realised that he was seeing what the buzzard was seeing. He lay back on the grass again and looked to the sky. There were about twenty herring gulls wheeling and calling against the deep blue of a beautiful Scottish July day. It was warm and there was a pleasant breeze, which always helped to keep the biting midges away from the coast. Midges, the scourge of the highlands and islands of Scotland, relentless, annoying biting insects that can swarm in their millions on a still day, making it deeply unpleasant to stay in the same place. Mr McBride never ceased to amuse himself by reminding everyone that it is only the female that bites.

Callum tried to project his mind into that of one of the gulls, but nothing seemed to be happening.

"What's happening?" asked Emma.

"Nothing" Callum snapped. "I can't do it."

"Were you taking anything this morning?" asked Emma.

"You sound like my brother," said Callum, "and no, I wasn't 'taking' anything."

"Well what were you thinking about this morning when it happened?" said Emma sounding a bit exasperated.

"I wasn't thinking about anything. I was just wondering what it would be like to be the buzzard," said Callum beginning to feel a bit put upon.

"Well have you tried that?" asked Emma.

"Well..."

27

"Well, try it then," said Emma, obviously exasperated now.

"Alreet, calm yoursen," said Callum.

He lay back again and fixed his eyes on one particular gull. He was still a bit annoyed at Emma so he said in a singsong voice "I wonder what it would be like to be a gull" and nothing happened.

"Don't say it out loud," said Emma in a slightly hoity-toity voice, "and it's not a password, if it is going to work at all I would imagine that you actually have to think it, not just say it."

Wow she's bossy, thought Callum, but he did as he was asked and tried to wonder what it would be like to be the gull. As he wondered he started to feel sick and then, just like before, he felt disorientated, like he had been spinning around and around. He felt dizzy as his eyesight swam back into focus. He was high up over the island and he could see himself and Emma. He could also see that the boat now had waves lapping up to the bow and if he didn't get back to it soon, it would be taken by the tide and he and Emma would be marooned. His eyesight was keen but the gull darted its eyes backwards and forwards in a confusing way, presumably looking for food. He could hear the continual calls of the other gulls and he found himself distracted by the changing flight path, there was nothing steady here like the buzzard. There was no urgency in the hunt for food in the gull.

Callum was becoming aware of another feeling. It wasn't akin to anything that he had felt before. It was a rushing, like stroking or being stroked… but not quite, it wasn't soft or gentle. Callum realised that it was the sensation of flying, the air currents flowing over the feathers on the gull's back and wings. Now the dizziness and nausea had gone Callum was beginning to enjoy himself. Although quite scared of heights in his own body Callum felt quite safe being carried along by the gull.

After a while, he began to get worried about the boat that he could see beginning to lift at the stern as the tide came in, and he decided that he had had enough. He could also see Emma shaking his body, and now she was slapping his face. That looked like it could really hurt. All he had to do now was transfer back into his own body… So all he had to do now was transfer back into his own body… How? He tried to concentrate on being in his own body but it didn't seem to work. He tried wondering what it would be like to be back in his own body but again there was nothing. He looked through the gull's eyes and he could see the boat fully afloat now and he could hear Emma shouting up to the gull…to him presumably, but he seemed powerless to do anything about it. Even worse was that the gull seemed to be bored of hovering over the Island and was heading back towards Fionnphort. Callum could sense the island, and Emma and Iain's boat was getting further and further away. What would happen when the gull was out of sight? Would his consciousness remain trapped in the gull forever? Or would it simply cease to be? Would he die in this gull?

Just then the gull wheeled in mid-air and he could see quite how far he was away from Emma, he could no longer see her on the island. As he realised this he started to feel very light-headed and disjointed. He could feel his consciousness fading away. Was this the end? Was he dying?

Callum woke to find that Emma was smacking him on his cheek really hard, and by the feel of it, she had been doing it for quite a while. She may only have been a twelve year old girl but she packed quite a punch.

"Will ye get off!" shouted Callum. "That hurts!"

"Why did you stay up there so long?" said Emma. Callum thought he noticed a quaver in her voice and were those tear tracks down her face? "You scared me! Your body went all cold and floppy. I thought you'd died! Why did you stay up there for so long?"

"Do you think I wanted to? I couldn't get back...the boat!" Callum leapt to his feet and ran back down to the beach as he remembered seeing the boat afloat, and a very good thing it was that he did remember. The boat was a few feet from the beach gently drifting away. He waded in and caught it just in time. Emma was just behind him.

The trip back to Fionnphort took ten minutes and was uneventful. Both of them seemed a bit overawed by the whole gull experience and Callum found that it had drained him. After a few minutes, he started thinking about the entire afternoon and how he had spilt his guts to Emma, what was more, she had seemed to believe him!

"Emma," said Callum, "how did you know about that teletransference stuff?"

"My dad" replied Emma, "he writes books about religious communities which is why my parents chose Mull for a holiday house. He thinks that some of the fundamentalist beliefs are a bit like Father Christmas, the Tooth Fairy or telekinesis and telepathy. He talks about all of that stuff and I guess I picked it up."

"Maybe we should tell your dad…"

"No!" Emma interrupted sharply. "He studies it, he doesn't believe any of it. He wouldn't believe you."

"Do you believe me?" Callum was almost scared of hearing the answer. This morning he had thought he was going mad and yet if this MOST ANNOYING girl believed him he thought that he could persuade himself that he wasn't going mad. Suddenly it seemed really important that Emma should believe him.

"Do you believe me?" Callum pushed for an answer, and the silence, while he waited, was almost unbearable. As the seconds ticked by Callum found himself getting angrier and angrier. Why did he care what this silly girl thought? He didn't want to take her out in the boat anyway, it was her who pushed him to be the gull, it was her who came to bug him when he was on top of the hill that morning, it was her who interfered with his boat launch, it was her who came up with all that teletransferance rubbish… "Don't believe me then…I don't care what you think anyway!"

Emma looked hurt by this outburst and Callum felt sorry immediately. "I was just about to say that I did believe you. I've already told you that I always say what I think and sometimes I need time to decide what I think. Now I'm not so sure. You seem to be quite unstable and that is a well-known side effect of someone taking drugs."

Callum's initial instinct to apologise for his outburst evaporated from his tongue and he sat looking sullenly over Emma's shoulder.

"You can jump out now," he said as they pulled up at the quayside. Emma jumped out, took off her lifejacket, and without a backward glance, she walked up the quay and mingled with the few tourists who were waiting for the ferry to Iona. He last saw her with her head down, walking slowly back towards her parents' house. Callum had failed in his earlier promise to himself not to do something that he would later be ashamed of. Oh well, he was only human. He moored the boat and started up the hill to home.

Callum found that his legs were shaking with exhaustion. He guessed that it was a result of his unbelievable day. So far he had been a buzzard, a gull, and a dying rabbit, he'd met an annoying girl, and had almost wrecked Iain's boat, and it was only 5.30 pm! If his holiday continued at this rate he would be exhausted and sectioned to a mental hospital by his birthday next week!

Thankfully normality returned as soon as he walked through the door of his ferryman's cottage home.

"Cal, is it you?" shouted Mrs McBride,

"Aye ma."

"Is it true what they're saying? Have ye spint the whole afternoon wi a lass?"

"That didne tek long te get aroond" Callum replied.

"A wee English lass…a wee bit odd I heard."

Callum decided to leave the conversation at that. He knew from experience that Mrs McBride would be demanding a minute-by-minute account of his whole day if he didn't end it soon.

"Aye, and I heard ye came close to wrecking yon boat a Iain's an all!" Just what Callum needed. Now Mr McBride was joining in. Callum reckoned it was Seamus Dougherty on the ferry who had squealed on him. Seamus was a mate of Mr McBride's who had always paid an interest in Callum's fate, as it was him who had found Callum. Since then Mr McBride and Seamus seemed almost inseparable. Seamus even came to Christmas lunch. Callum wasn't sure whether he liked him or not. On this occasion, Seamus had been driving the ferry when Emma had saved his bacon and had obviously ratted out on him to his dad.

"Aye the engine wouldne start, a wee bit o' dirt in the fuel I reckon."

"If ye say so." said Mr McBride sounding as if he didn't believe this for a second.

Tea consisted of sausage and potatoes and Callum found himself hungrier than he would have thought possible.

"Ye've got yoursen an appetite lad. Is it the wee lass that has ye hungry is it?" enquired Mr McBride. Callum knew from watching Iain go through the same that sullen silence would do him no good and the best defence against this sort of teasing was an attack.

"Aye it must be. She canna get enough of me so I'm off oot to see her now," he replied. Mr McBride replied with a great deep guffaw with his bass gravely voice teasing Callum as he headed out of the door.

As it was July, the sun wouldn't set until 11 o'clock and as he wasn't at school he had no particular bedtime. There were different dangers in Mull to other places. Crime was very low. If someone burgled your house, the getaway was 32 miles down a single track lane. There was very little violence, and as everyone knew everybody else, any crime that there was, got solved quickly. Callum then had his freedom until dark. After it got dark there were other dangers; cliffs, waves, tides, and bogs, and the threat of these increased enormously after dark so that was when Callum had to be home.

Callum found himself wandering through the village. Nothing was open, (except the pub which he wasn't allowed to go into without his mum or dad). He crossed the main road in and out of the village to the road to where the big ferry from Craignure took him to school in Oban every Sunday in term time. He wandered up past the Columba centre where there was a display of the history of St Columba, and a car park where everyone left their car when they went to Iona for more than a day. As usual, he could hear a car alarm going off. No doubt set off by a sheep scratching itself on a bumper. There would be another tourist with a flat battery tomorrow and another long drive for Dermot who was the AA man based in Craignure. As he walked, he went over the events of the day and he felt he had been a bit mean to Emma. Yes, she was annoying and had stuck her nose into his business, but she HAD saved his bacon at the slip AND said that she believed him. He couldn't think of anyone else, except perhaps Andrew, who would believe him. Maybe he should try being nice to the only person who knew and did believe him. He found himself outside a traditional single-storey Scottish cottage. It had been built the previous winter and everyone in the village had spent more time than was healthy speculating on who had bought it. Morag in the shop had finally tracked down the architect via the builders and found out it was an Englishman, Professor Higgins. There had been great hilarity in the village as this is the name of the main character in the musical My

Fair Lady (Elisa Dolittle). The hilarity had been accompanied by lots of terrible impersonations of a cockney accent. There isn't a lot to do in Fionnphort in the long evenings of the short bleak winter days. As it turned out, Professor Higgins was not from London but from Oxford where he was a Professor of Religious Studies at Balliol College. The first time he came into the shop in the village he had managed to upset three people without even noticing. Oh well, thought Callum, here goes. He knocked on the bright blue door and waited, blushing slightly. The door opened and Callum was relieved to see that it was Emma who answered.

"I wondered how long it would take you to get here."

"What?" This was not what Callum had expected. He had half expected Emma to refuse to talk to him, but he hadn't expected this.

"I accept your apology."

"What? What apology…how did you know I was coming to apologise?" stammered Callum.

"It's obvious," said Emma, "you were horrible to me, but you have been brought up well so you have come to apologise. I am saving you the embarrassment of actually having to do it."

This was too much for Callum. OK so he had been horrible, and he had come to apologise but did Emma have to be so…so…KNOW IT ALL about it.

"Maybe I've changed my mind and I don't want to apologise now," he growled.

"Well that's up to you," said Emma "but if you are going to be so silly then I won't tell you everything I've learned about teletransference."

She just stood there in the doorway. Waiting.

"Alright," he mumbled. It hurt to say. It hurt to see the little smile on her face, but it would hurt even more to go home without learning what Emma had found out about teletransference.

"My mum and dad are out at the restaurant so you can come upstairs to my bedroom." Emma said this with no intonation in her voice either suggestive or otherwise. Callum was not experienced in dealing with girls but over the last year he had spent more and more time thinking about them. What he did remember was the time Mrs McBride had caught his elder sister, Isla in her bedroom with one of her many boyfriends. She had been 17 and the poor lad had only gone in to help with carrying a case downstairs, but to hear Mrs McBride, you would think that they had been caught being 'inappropriate' (school word) or 'making out' Isla's words, or 'at it' (Iain's words)! Callum wasn't sure about girls, but he was very wary of entering the bedroom of one of them.

Curiosity overcame his concerns and he went into the house, which was nicely decorated in a modern way and Callum had a chance to see that they had Sky and a huge plasma screen TV before he was whisked upstairs into the single loft room. Isla's room had been all pink and soft toys with a few books and posters of One Direction, and he expected the same from Emma's room. How wrong was he!

As Emma entered the room Callum thought he had gone to heaven. THIS was the bedroom that Callum wanted. 38" Wall-mounted flat-screen TV, 21" LCD flatscreen PC with the latest Wi-Fi colour laser printer/

scanner combo, X-Box, Sky TV and what was that in the back of the PC base unit? It was, it was a wireless network box that could only mean superfast broadband. Callum knew that the local exchange had only been made superfast fibre broadband compliant the month before after pressure on British Telecom by the Scottish Parliament. Emma must be the first person in the village to get superfast broadband.

"Wow" was all that Callum could say.

"They're guilt gifts," said Emma seeing the look on Callum's face.

"My parents feel guilty about bringing me up here away from all of my friends for the whole summer, so they have made me, and themselves, feel better by buying me all this stuff. As I didn't have any friends anyway, it's quite a good deal."

"I wish my parents felt a bit guilty about me," muttered Callum while looking wistfully at the X-Box. "Why don't you have any friends?"

"Why do I make you angry all the time?" was the quiet, wistful reply.

After a few moments of awkward silence, Emma sighed and sat at the PC. She pulled up an archive of web pages that she had been viewing earlier and summarised what she had found while showing them to Callum.

"I was wrong earlier about teletransference. I thought it had been reported when people had been taking drugs like LSD, Acid or Ecstasy. Apparently, it was reported when scientists were trying to develop drugs in the 80s and 90s that could enhance a human's natural intelligence and senses like touch and eyesight and hearing. Apparently the program was stopped after worrying side effects were found on the soldiers who were the guinea pigs for the tests. One of the side effects was claimed to be teletransference. It has only been reported between the soldiers in the test labs and has led to madness in a few. There has been an ongoing legal battle for the last 10 years because the soldiers are trying to get damages. The defence is that teletransference doesn't exist and that the soldiers are making it up. None of them can do it now so no one believes them." Emma had hardly drawn breath when she continued; "What drugs have you been taking?"

"That's the third time you have accused me of taking drugs and for the LAST TIME, I don't do drugs."

"Have you ever done drugs?"

"Apart from ten cigarettes two years ago no!" exclaimed Callum "I can see why you don't have any friends!" Callum couldn't believe how quickly this Emma could rub him up the wrong way! Aaaaagh!

"… Sorry".

Callum realised that he had apologised (or at least had his apology accepted) more times in a single day than probably the whole of the previous year. He had NEVER met anyone so annoying.

"That's OK," said Emma. "But teletransference has only ever been reported when people have been taking experimental drugs!"

"Well I haven't and I am getting fed up with you saying I have," replied Callum.

"I didn't say that you have, I asked if you have" protested Emma.

"A very fine distinction if you ask me" grunted Callum.

"Have you noticed that when you are with me your Scottish accent is less pronounced?" Emma said completely out of the blue.

"What?" Callum was finding it difficult to follow where this girl was going. "What's that got to do with it?"

"I reckon your real mother must have been English. Babies learn the basics of their language at a very early age you know, and that pattern can be imprinted long before they can talk themselves."

"How do you know that I was adopted?" Callum demanded?

Without answering Emma played a clip of a newscast that she had downloaded from the internet. The news was from the Monday after Callum had been found and it gave the basic details of how he had been found and appealed for information. The clip looked strange with the different haircuts and clothes. It was all about him although it didn't mention him by name.

"How did you know it was me?" Callum demanded. "And why were you researching me?" Callum could feel his anger growing. Who did she think she was looking him up on the internet?

"Sorry," said Emma. "I was just interested; I didn't mean to make you cross. You get cross a lot."

"Only when I'm with you. Anyway, you didn't say how you knew it was me."

"You are the right age, you look nothing like your family, and you can teletransfer into animals. Who else could it be?"

This was the first time Callum had even considered putting the two things together…maybe this teletranferance thing was genetic…

There was a noise downstairs. "That's my parents home." Emma interrupted his silence and he realised that he must have been just sitting looking at the blank screen.

"You'd better be going."

"Right," said Callum. "I'll be off then, thanks for this. I'll come and get you in the morning." Emma said nothing but smiled.

Emma and Callum scuttled down the stairs and ran straight into Professor and Mrs Higgins. Not really sure of how he should act at 10 pm in someone else's house when they came home from a restaurant, Callum said nothing and stood directly behind Emma. He wasn't exactly hiding, but if they didn't see him that would be fine.

"Hello Angel!" said Emma's mother, "are you feeling better?"

Having not thought about it before, Callum was beginning to get an inkling as to why Emma had been left behind when her parents went to the restaurant.

"Who's that?" was the imperious question put in a slightly fierce tone by the ever so pompous looking Professor Higgins. He must have rivalled Mr McBride for size but he seemed much more 'squidgy'. He had a fat round belly and jowls that wobbled when he spoke. He seemed quite old to have a twelve year old daughter. He was dressed in… Callum just couldn't believe it…in full English tweeds! Were those jodphurs?

"I am unhappy about him being in our house," he said not appearing to talk to anyone in particular, and then definitely turning to Callum. "Please leave."

"Now don't be rude to our young guest Henry," chastised his wife. "It is quite late now," she said turning to Callum. "If you aren't doing anything for lunch tomorrow come around at 11.30 and Emma can introduce you to us then."

Callum had sense enough to know that this would be a good time to leave. Without speaking he turned to leave and before he had even closed the door behind him he could hear the Professor remonstrating with his daughter about; 1) lying to them about feeling ill and 2) sneaking a boy into the house so late. As he walked away from the cottage he could hear Emma protesting her innocence that she didn't lie, she was just feeling better now, and that she didn't know Callum was going to knock on the door until he did and she could hardly turn him away. It was interesting to learn that even the tomboy daughters of professors would lie to them barefacedly! Hang on, didn't Emma say that she never lied? Still, it meant that Callum felt uneasy about going back the following lunchtime and meeting them properly.

When he got home, he said goodnight, fell into bed exhausted and hoped he didn't have his dream again. Just as he was dropping off to sleep he realised that he was smiling. Emma took some getting used to, but maybe the next two weeks until Andrew got back wouldn't be so bad after all.

Chapter 3

Tuesday Morning

Callum woke with a start.

Wow, no dream! Plus he found he was feeling much more content than recent mornings. When he questioned himself he discovered that it was because he was looking forward to going back to Emma's house. The stuff she had in her room was incredible! He could find out about all sorts of things. He had used the internet to do research at school, but he had never been allowed to look at anything he wanted. And it was too slow in the shop where you could rent a public PC, paying by the 15 minutes. His parents didn't see the need for the internet, so he lived in a house with no internet at all. He did have a cast-off pay as you go mobile from Iain but he couldn't afford the data and who was he going to call anyway? That reminded him, he needed to e-mail Andrew.

After getting up, dressing, and passing up the offer of mackerel from Mrs McBride, Callum hurried to the shop. There was only one shop; 'The Crossing Shop' in Fionnphort, and it served many purposes. Smaller than many corner shops around the country, it housed the grocery store, the gift shop, the post office, the sweet shop, the hardware shop, the off-licence, the bookshop and what Callum was most interested in, the internet café.

A fairly recent innovation in the shop, there were two PCs with internet connectivity that could be booked for 15 minutes at a time, although Callum didn't normally bother to book.

"Gud morning Morag" said Callum as he went through the shop, "Is there anyone on the PC?"

"Help yoursen Cal" said Morag who was serving Mrs McDougall (the biggest gossip that had ever lived; rumour had it that she knew so much, she must be connected electronically to Google).

Callum logged on while thinking that it would be nice to have superfast broadband and that if she let him he could do this from Emma's room. He smiled at the faded sign on top of the PC "Superfast Broadband coming soon!", it had been there as long as he could remember and last time he ran Google's speed check the shop connection was downloading at only 2Mb/s. When he logged on to his Hotmail account he found he had three e-mails. The first was from Andrew telling him all about his holiday so far. The second was from a girl at school who liked Callum but who he was trying to keep clear of. Her name was Kirsty and she had the worst bad breath you could

43

imagine. She was also one of the least popular girls in school. Callum had given her his e-mail address out of pity. He knew that you shouldn't dislike someone just because they have bad breath, but he found it difficult to even talk to her without gagging. As he was reading her banal e-mail he concluded that life was tough and he promptly deleted it.

The third was the most intriguing. It was from Iain asking Callum to tell Mrs McBride that he would be arriving for a week from the coming Saturday (it was Tuesday today). What was intriguing was that Iain wasn't expected back for months as he had only just visited. Callum replied saying that he had got the e-mail and would tell his mum and asking if Iain was bringing his girlfriend back, (Mrs McBride would want to know whether to make up the spare room or not). Almost straight away, Callum got the reply that Iain would be working on the Island. Callum knew that as Iain was an islander he always got the CID jobs on Mull but usually this meant staying in Tobermory on the other end of the island.

So there was CID business in Fionnphort or possibly Bunessan…interesting… Callum wondered if Mrs McDougall knew this yet…he reckoned she did and he laughed to himself.

Callum replied promising to tell his mum (who didn't hold with this new-fangled computer talk), "What's wrong wi' the telephone or e'en a letter?" Callum remembered her saying when Iain tried to persuade his parents to get a PC. Iain had turned to Callum, shrugged, raised his eyes to the sky and said, "Sorry Boat Boy, but I did try."

Callum snapped out of his reverie realising that he still hadn't e-mailed Andrew and he would shortly have to leave for Emma's or he would be late. He thought that Professor Higgins probably wasn't too hot on tardiness, and after last night he didn't want to alienate him even more.

Andrew,

I can transfer my mind into animals and I've met a girl called Emma.

No, that won't do… Andrew was bound to get the wrong idea about Emma.

Andrew,

Yesterday, I got eaten by a buzzard while I was a rabbit and I spent most of the day and some of the evening with a weird girl called Emma.

No, still not going to work.

Andrew,

I nearly crashed Iain's boat and ended up taking a new girl to Eilean Annraidh, where I occupied the mind of a gull while my body lay with the girl on the beach.

Whichever way he wrote it, it made it sound like he had a new girlfriend and that was so not true. Oh, and of course, he sounded completely insane as well.

Andrew,

Met a new girl in Fionnphort, minging. Lots to tell you about my weird dreams. See you soon.

Callum

PS Iain has lent me his boat… Cool.

That would have to do or he would be late, Emma certainly wasn't a minger, but if he said anything more complimentary Andrew would think that he was sweet on her.

It was only 150 metres from the shop to Emma's house yet it seemed to take an age. Callum couldn't stop thinking about how the Professor had been cross with him last night. Maybe, he wouldn't let Callum in. Maybe he wouldn't let Emma out. Maybe he would come round to the house and speak to Mr McBride about how Callum had been in Emma's room at 10 o'clock at night. Callum was getting butterflies just thinking about the looks that Mrs McBride would give him.

Anyway, he was here now and there was only one way to find out. He leant forward to knock at the newly painted blue door but at that very moment, the door opened.

"You're late," said Emma.

It was amazing. From anyone else, it would sound reproachful, but from Emma it was just a statement. He was getting used to it so he thought he would try it back.

"Aye, I am" Callum replied.

"Come in." She didn't bat an eyelid. She was definitely a little strange.

"Hello Callum," said Mrs Higgins. "It is very nice to see you. Come in and sit down."

Callum sat at the kitchen table nervously looking around.

"Don't worry dear," said Mrs Higgins, astutely interpreting the look that Callum had given. "The Professor is in his study and he's unlikely to remember lunchtime. He gets absorbed with his work so you will be eating with Emma and me."

Following this Callum relaxed and found he really liked Emma's mum. She had been a teacher, until they moved up to Mull, working with Asperger's children. Mrs Higgins then spent a long time describing the symptoms of Asperger's syndrome which sometimes include an inability to read social clues and a literal approach to language. If it had been Callum that his mum had been talking about he would have been cringing with embarrassment, but Emma didn't seem to even notice that they were really talking about her. It seemed really strange to Callum but he thought that she really didn't notice until she said; "Don't labour the point mum, Callum's quite bright really."

Mrs Higgins looked at Callum and raised an eyebrow.

"I understand," Callum told Mrs Higgins.

"Good lad, I knew you would."

"Of course he understands, you speak very clearly, why wouldn't he understand?" asked Emma.

A little while passed, and at least two of the people around the table didn't know what to say.

In desperation to fill the awkward silence "Why did you move up here?" asked Callum. He knew that Emma had told him it was because of her father's work, but he was struggling for conversation so was really surprised when Mrs Higgins said, "Hasn't Emma told you? We had a spot

47

of bother at Emma's school and we all decided to spend some time up here before Emma starts in a new school in September. I'm surprised Emma didn't tell you."

The rest of the meal was uneventful and Callum spent most of the time wondering what Emma had done which required the whole family to buy a house several hundred miles away! He couldn't wait to ask her.

After lunch had finished and Callum had offered to wash up, (an offer Mrs Higgins had declined, much to Callum's relief). Emma stood at the door with Callum, obviously uncomfortable.

"What's wrong Emma?"

"I want to spend the afternoon with you but mum tells me it's rude to ask so I am waiting for you to ask me but you might not."

"I can see why that might be troubling" said Callum. "Would you fancy a walk to Erraid to see the seals?"

"That would be great," said Emma, the conflict in her face receding.

It was a long walk past Fidden Farm where all the campers came every summer, at least a couple of miles, and Callum lost no time in asking Emma about her school.

"I thought you said that you came to Mull because of your dad?"

"Yes."

"But your mum said it was because of your school. I thought you always told the truth!"

"I do always tell the truth. You asked why we came to Mull. We came to Mull because of my dad's work. Mum told you why we left Oxford. That was because of me."

"Well go on then. Tell me what you did!"

"I hacked into the MI6 computer mainframe in my IT lesson."

"You what?" exclaimed Callum.

"I hacked into the MI6 computer mainframe in my IT lesson."

Callum didn't know what to say. He didn't have any clue how you could even start to do such a thing. He was silenced by the enormity of Emma's crime.

"What did they do to you?"

"Nothing. The school said that they were 'no longer able to meet my educational needs' so I have to move schools. MI6 said they were grateful that I had exposed a loophole in their security, and asked me to give them a ring when I was looking for a job. They were very nice you know."

"Are you sure it was the MI6 computer and not just a website?" asked Callum still struggling to comprehend such a thing.

"I believed you, you know," replied Emma, "and being able to hack into a secure system that wasn't as secure as they thought, is much more likely than being able to teletransfer into the mind of an animal."

"Aye, you're right, I s'pose it is. What were you looking for?"

"Nothing, in particular. It was my teacher's fault. I had done all of my work and I was asking what to do. Some of the other pupils were running riot and Mum said that she only told me to do it to get me to leave her alone."

"Said to do what?" asked Callum imagining the scene

only too easily.

"She said I could do something to show how good I was at IT. Something original that no one else had done. I surfed a while and found a chat room for hackers where one hacker had challenged another to hack into MI6 so I did it instead."

"How did you even know how to start?" asked Callum, completely bewildered now.

"Well, first you have to find a way of getting into their system, past their firewall. In my case, I found that one of the operatives had simply asked their networked workstation to send a fax. I don't know why they were sending a fax…it's pretty outdated now and the security isn't as good as with other comms. As soon as the computer connected to an online fax server I was able to track the IP address and take advantage of the operating system vulnerability on the 1098 port. I got in, had a look around, left a calling card and left. I went back to the chat room and told the hacker what I'd done. He didn't believe me until they arrested him and his friend. They were let off with a warning."

Callum wasn't sure he dared to ask, "What was your calling card?"

I wrote a note on the screen of the person who sent the fax telling them my initials. I also told them how I got in and I made it so that the computer user couldn't use their workstation until they entered a password. As soon as they contacted me I gave them the password."

"What was the password?" asked Callum with his mouth hanging open.

"PASSWORD," said Emma.

Callum was dumbfounded by this revelation and he found that he looked at Emma with a whole new respect. Weird she definitely was, but how clever was she? Certainly cleverer than him, and Iain, and Andrew…maybe she was the cleverest person he had ever met.

They walked largely in companionable silence. Callum was used to trekking all over the Ross of Mull to find the best places to swim, or to watch hares boxing in the spring, or occasionally to see the dolphins as they swam in the sound, but Emma wasn't and he was secretly impressed that she could keep up with him. He was also extremely grateful that she didn't seem to feel the need to talk all the time so for much of the time they just walked in a comfortable silence.

When they got there, they sat at the top of the hill overlooking the bay and the island where the seals were basking. The sky was blue, the sun was out and the bay was picture-postcard stuff.

"So what animals can you teletransfer into?"

"What?"

"What animals can you teletransfer into?"

"Do you not want to take a wee second to look at the view?" asked Callum, bemused.

"Yes, I've looked at the view," said Emma "but which animals you can teletransfer into is a bit more important, don't you think?"

"Yes, I suppose so." Callum had been dreading raising the subject again. What if it didn't work, or worse still… what if it did?

51

"You'll need to work out how to get back into your own body."

"Why? All I have to do is not teletransfer and then I'll be normal like you."

"You really think I'm normal?"

The big brown eyes looked quizzically at him, unblinking and demanding.

"Aye…well…aye, of course yer normal,"

"You're lying. You think I'm strange." Emma said this without even looking sad. How do you say that without being sad?

"Well, maybe I think you might be a bit weird…but only a tiny bit…and in a really good way." Callum cringed as he said it, but Emma seemed satisfied.

"Most people think I'm weird. Some of my teachers say it is because I am gifted."

"What are you gifted at?"

"School stuff. I'm actually quite brilliant."

How did she say that without sounding big-headed?

"And that means that I know that you should be practising getting out of the heads of animals you get into."

"Well I suppose I could try that oyster catcher."

"Go on then."

Callum focused on the bird flying below him and concentrated on what it might be like to be flying so fast over the beach towards the kids on the cliff on the other side of the bay. He hadn't noticed them before. As he concentrated he felt the same nausea and disorientation (was it less now?) and then he was there, flying over the beach. The feeling of speed and freedom as the wind ruffled his feathers was indescribably exciting. Callum had once been to a theme park just south of Glasgow (the furthest south he had ever been) and the thrill of the rollercoaster was nothing compared to the thrill he was experiencing now. It was strange to be able to feel his wings and not his arms. The oyster catcher was beginning to pull away from where Callum's body and Emma were sitting and Callum tried to get back to his body. He tried to focus on what it must be like to be Callum, but even as he was trying he felt the lack of commitment. He knew what it was like to be Callum. In this moment he would far rather be the oyster catcher. The oyster catcher had wheeled and was back facing the other way and Callum had a good view of Emma shouting and gesticulating madly. Keep your hair on, thought Callum, I've only been up here a minute, until he saw that Emma was pointing, not at him, but across the bay. Callum felt a tiny bit sick when he realised that he could look that way at the same time with both images slightly overlapping. What he saw was a nightmare in action. One of the children he had seen just a moment ago, who had been playing on the top of the cliff was right on the lip holding on to the grass. She must have slipped and just caught herself. The kid can't have been more than about five years old. She was crying, as were the other two who were just out of reach. Callum could see what was presumably the mother running towards the cliff to help her children but it was obvious that the kid would never be able to hold on for long enough. What could he do to help? Even if he was in his own body there would be nothing he could do, he was all the way across the other side of the bay. Luckily the oyster catcher had peeled off from the rest of its small flock and was flying towards the kid in just such a way that Callum could see exactly what was going on. As he got closer he could see that the kid was half hanging over a vertical cliff that fell three or four metres into about six metres of water. Thank heaven the tide was in and there were no rocks. At least the fall probably wouldn't kill her. The big question was whether she could swim or not.

It was inevitable that the grass clasped between her petrified fingers would only hold for so long. As it eventually had to, first the right hand gave and then with the extra weight, the grass in her left hand gave. Callum watched as if in slow motion the girl fell backwards, spreadeagled, the long four metres straight down to the icy Atlantic waters, still clutching the grass in both her tiny hands.

The oyster catcher landed on the water ten metres from where the girl went in, only a couple of seconds after she hit. This is a very helpful oyster catcher thought Callum briefly. He was worried as she made a very loud smacking sound when she hit the water and went down what seemed a very long way. Callum waited for the little girl to re-surface. He waited for what seemed a very long time. A very long time indeed.

She was going to die. Callum knew it. There was an unstoppable inevitability about it. She had fallen too far, was wearing too many clothes, the water was too cold and she had gone too deep. Callum could see her mother, still not up to the top of the cliff, and her father struggling 200 metres away in the shallows. Callum knew that a child that size would be brain dead inside two to three minutes. She had already been under for two and no one was going to get to her quickly enough. If Callum had been here in his own body, he could have got to her. One of the advantages of growing up on the island was that he was an excellent swimmer. But he wasn't here in his own body was he? He was here as an oyster catcher. Great for flying. Rubbish for diving.

Hold on…why was he here? He could hear the other oyster catchers way back on the beach. Why had this one come to exactly where he wanted it to? Surely he couldn't… If he could then… He knew that he only had seconds to act. It had to work!

Callum could see the island where the seals basked and he could see the two metre, half a tonne, bull seal. Be the seal, be the seal!

He felt nauseous, disorientated and then he was basking on the rock. Yes! He was the seal! Now all he had to do was get it to do what he wanted. He had to get off the rock and dive. Dive to where the little girl's life force was ebbing into the sea like so many others before her.

The seal heaved itself in to the water and swam. Wow, what swimming. This was an animal designed for this task. No cold, perfect vision and the speed! It took less than a few seconds for the seal to cross the 50 metres and swim to the bottom. Callum could see the girl, floating just above the bottom, her pretty dress clinging to her legs. So noisy and THERE in life and now in death, so absent. Callum was certain that he was too late but he had to try. The seal opened its crushingly strong jaws and closed them so gently on the back of the dress. With one flick of his mighty tail they shot up to and out of the surface. Callum hoped that the girl would start to breathe on her own but she didn't. He feared it was too late. Callum swam the girl as quickly as he could towards her father who was still fighting his way through the shallows. Callum felt nervous as the water got shallower, but he didn't drop the girl until he got within half a metre of the father. The father was standing looking with his mouth open as a huge bull seal gently dropped his daughter at his feet. He grabbed the girl and without trying to get the girl back to shore he started Artificial Ventilation (AV), the scientific term for mouth to mouth resuscitation. Watching the man work from a safe distance Callum felt himself willing the little girl to breathe. The father obviously had been trained in AV but until she coughed, spluttered, and started crying (with her dad crying just as loudly), he hadn't felt much hope.

The girl was alive. Now that felt GOOD! The girl was alive. The girl was alive and he was able to control the animals he was in! He was able to control the animals he teletransferred into!

Without realising it the seal was now back on his island basking in the sun and Callum looked back towards Emma and thought I must tell Emma.

He sat up almost immediately back in his body. The transfer itself seemed to be getting easier and easier and this time he had instigated it himself. He wasn't sure how, he'd have to work that one out later.

"That was you wasn't it?" asked Emma.

"Yes. I teletransferred into the oyster catcher and then the seal," replied Callum.

"You told me that you couldn't control the animal you transferred into," said Emma.

"Aye, I know, but I just sort of did when I wanted to be near the wee girl. Once I'd realised that I could, I transferred to the seal and saved her!"

"Yes."

"What do you mean, "Yes"?" asked Callum, who was beginning to feel that there wasn't enough praise for saving the girl. He'd get a medal or something for this, maybe even a reward and then he could buy himself a PC and broadband.

"Callum?"

"Yes?"

"How many people know about what you can do?" asked Emma.

"Only you and me," replied Callum, with a quizzical note to his voice. "Why?"

"Because grown-ups won't believe you, you know. They'll say you have been taking drugs or that you are mentally unstable. That's what the UK and the US governments have been saying about those soldiers who were experimented on. It's just so unbelievable."

"Well it did happen. I saved that kid's life. Why shouldn't I tell everyone? What harm can it do?"

"Callum, think about it. If you could demonstrate what you can do to a court then the governments would lose their case and it would cost them millions of pounds in compensation. There may be people out there who don't want that to happen. Nasty people."

"You read too many adventure books you do. Life isn't like that!" said Callum who was beginning to feel the glory slipping away from him and was getting more and more irate.

"There's no point getting cross with me. I just don't think that you should tell anyone else about what you can do!"

Even as he said it Callum knew that it was a mean and nasty thing to say but he was angry and wanted to hit out, with Emma being the nearest person. "You just don't want me to tell anyone else because you've never had a friend to share a secret with before."

A few long seconds passed with Callum feeling even more guilty about what he had just said.

"Sorry Callum," said Emma.

"What?"

"Sorry Callum," said Emma again.

"What are you saying sorry for?" said Callum incredulously. "It was me who was horrid. Not you!"

"Oh." said Emma sadly, "Shouldn't I have said sorry? I'm learning what to do when people are angry with me, and my mum says that a good thing to do is apologise. You were angry so I apologised. If you were being horrid then you should apologise to me."

"Aaargh! What sort of weirdo are you?" demanded Callum playfully.

Emma's face fell and she looked like she was going to start to cry. What now thought Callum.

"That was abusive. I don't need to take abuse from anyone, so I'm going home" said Emma getting up to go.

"Wait!" shouted Callum. "I was nasty the first time, not the second time. I was playing when I called you a weirdo. Wait!"

But Emma carried on walking leaving Callum at a loss to explain what had gone wrong now, and with the euphoria of saving the girl evaporating he found that he was really, really, tired.

Having dragged his feet the two and a half miles back to Fionnphort, Callum decided to pop into the Crossing Shop for some much needed confectionery and was unsurprised to discover that news of the rescue was all over the village. Apparently, it had been a miracle that a dolphin had held the girl up until her dad had got there. It looked like the father would come out of this as the hero with a bit part for a dolphin that wasn't even there. Callum didn't mind the dad getting some glory as he did do a great job on the resuscitation, but it seemed a bit unfair that the seal didn't get a mention.

Maybe Emma was right. Maybe he shouldn't tell anyone. Who would believe him? The soldiers who were suing the government. They would believe him. Maybe he should contact them. Even if he did, so what? What good would that do him or them?

In the end, Callum went home, had his tea and was in bed at a sensible time. He felt drained by his exertions. He lay awake for several minutes thinking about everything that had happened over the last few days. He felt sorry about the terms on which he had parted with Emma but there was nothing that he could do about that now.

Or was there?

Did he have enough energy to do this one last thing today?

Callum wrote a short note; *Sorry about today. See you tomorrow?*

He left the note on the windowsill, spotted a gull still flying around and concentrated hard. The familiar feeling of sickness, a bit like the feeling when you go too fast over a humpback bridge in a car, and disorientation, like when you spin around and around and around and then stop, hit him and he was flying. He concentrated on the note that he had left on the table and swooped in to pick it up. He flew straight to Emma's house and landed on her windowsill. He tapped once on the window, dropped the note and took off to watch. After a few seconds the window opened and Emma picked up the note.

"OK!" she shouted, looking at the wrong gull. Callum smiled, or tried to, is it possible for a seagull to even smile? Callum didn't know and the seagull...sorry Emma, the "gull" wasn't saying. He flew home, transferred into his own body that was thankfully lying in his bed with the full intention of going straight to sleep.

For the first time in many, many years Callum found himself thinking about his real mum. Why did she leave him? Who was she? What did she look like? Why had she been in Fionnphort? After she left him where did she go? Why did she leave him? Why did she leave him? Sleep eluded him for longer than it should have considering how tired he was.

"Callum! Time to get yoursen oot a bed!" shouted Mrs McBride.

"What's got in te you sleepy heed? I'll bet it's the wee lassie you've bin spending all your days with. Bring her back for tea tonight, why don't you."

"Mum you'll no like her. She's a wee bit tapped in the heed. She doesna understand everything and she says some weird stuff."

"The word in the village is that she's some sorta child genius."

"Aye, she's clever wi computers and that, but she canna talk sense."

"Tea tonight Callum," said Mrs McBide with a finality that brooked no argument. Some of Callum's friends at school had started to answer their parents back, but not Callum.

"Aye mum. I'll ask if it's OK."

By 11am, Callum was round at Emma's and he was invited in and shown into Emma's room where she was on the computer with reams of paper strewn around her room.

"So what are you looking at?" asked Callum.

"Did you know that there was quite a police investigation when you were found. Apparently there was some concern over a religious group on Iona. A few young women had disappeared in London and one came home saying that she had been on Iona and that there was an LSD manufacturing plant there."

Callum laughed. "Oh aye, and how on earth would you know that from the internet?"

"I'm not on the internet, except as a route in."

"A route into what?" Asked Callum, suddenly wishing that he didn't already know the answer.

"The National Crimes Computer in London has an outgoing fax link to all the police divisional headquarters around the country and whoever set up the security forgot about the operating system security susceptibility on the 1098 port. A lot of people forget about the 1098 port vulnerability. I could fix it from here but then I wouldn't be able to get back in so easily."

"You havne! You havne hacked the National Crime Computer! They'll crucify us!"

"They'll never track me I went through eight anonymous proxy servers all in different countries. Don't worry."

"Is that what you said when you got caught by MI6?" asked Callum incredulously.

Emma went quiet and, unusually for her said nothing.

"What is it?" Asked Callum.

"MI6 didn't catch me."

"I thought you said that you were excluded from school because you hacked into the MI6 computer?" accused Callum.

"I said that my school said they could no longer meet my educational needs because I hacked into the MI6 computer. I never said that they caught me."

"Well how did you get caught then?" demanded Callum.

"My dad phoned them," said Emma angrily. "I started the hack at school and finished it from my home computer. He did a scan of my PC while I was at school the next day and phoned them up. They didn't believe that it was me that hacked their computer until I gave them the password. They came round and were waiting for me after school. It was MI6 who bought me this computer because they took my old one away. They made me promise never to hack into their computers again."

"If your dad scanned your PC once, might he not do it again and then you'll get into at least as much trouble when he sees that you have hacked the police computer?" asked Callum.

"No he won't do that again," said Emma with some finality. "I don't allow him access anymore."

Callum didn't know what to say. Either Emma really was a genius or she was completely barking mad. Callum wasn't sure which he found scarier.

"What else did you find?" he asked, almost scared of the answer.

"Well there is a name that keeps coming up, both with regard to the court case against the servicemen, and the police investigation into the religious sect on Iona. There is a Doctor Christian Slack, a pharmacologist, who was part of the study in the eighties into 'superhumans' that used high doses of LSD that supposedly led to teletransference. He was definitely there when the experiments with the servicemen were going on and he was there on Iona when you were found. I am still looking to see if I can find out more about him. I am very confused because I can't seem to find his academic qualifications anywhere. Most people's thesis for their doctorate are online now, or at least some papers written by them, but he seems to be very shy. He has no criminal record, but he also hasn't registered to vote, and I cannot find any record of him paying tax."

"How can you find out about him paying tax?...no no, don't answer that. I am sure that I don't need to know." Callum muttered.

"I've also been looking for your mum, but I haven't found out much yet. Do you want me to carry on looking?"

"I'm not sure," said Callum quietly, "I never really thought about it… well I did think about it but I didn't want to know. What if she's dead? What if she isn't and she didn't want me? What if… just what if?"

"Well you won't know if you don't look. Mum said I shouldn't talk to you about it because it might be insensitive. Do you think I am insensitive to ask you if you want me to find your mother for you? I would want to find my real mother if she wasn't downstairs," said Emma with a rush.

"OK" said Callum, "keep looking but don't tell me if it is something bad."

"Can I ask my mum if it is something bad? I'm not very good at deciding," asked Emma.

"You rely on your mum a lot, don't you?" asked Callum.

"Yes," said Emma, and they went out.

Having cleared it with Emma's mum that Emma could come round for tea, they went out on Iain's boat around the coast to a secluded beach that you could only reach easily by boat. Called Market Bay, it was known locally as 'Royal Beach' as the young Princes Charles, Andrew, and Edward, apparently liked to swim there as they were unlikely to be bothered by the paparazzi. The beach was of pure white sand that came from the granite that underlies the Ross of Mull and gives it its unique flora and fauna. On either side of the sand are steep granite rock faces, topped by grass. To the back of the beach that narrows to a V are a few small sand dunes with a stream meandering through. Callum was convinced that this must be one of the most beautiful beaches in the world. On a day like today, with blue sky and a mild sea breeze, with unbroken views to the north west, taking in the island of Staffa and the Treshnish Isles, he knew it was one of the most stunning places in the world.

What Callum wasn't so sure about, was what he was doing here with Emma. In three short days she had become his confidante and the person with whom he spent all of his time. She was the only person who knew that he could teletransfer; it was her who had told him what it was that he was doing! It was Emma, not Andrew his best friend or his family that he was confiding all his secrets to. It was Emma that was looking to find out if anyone else could teletransfer, and Emma who was trying to find his real mum. What did he know about her? Only that she was seriously strange and that she was a bit of an uber nerd when it came to computers, oh, and that she had been excluded from school for hacking into the MI6 computer. He had seen for himself the information that had come from the police computer. This girl was a little bit scary.

Perhaps the thing that was scaring Callum more than anything else was the fact that he quite liked her. The girls at school were all a bit silly for Callum. They spent their time doing their hair and messaging their friends that were in the same room. They hung around in groups giggling and talking about the latest boy bands and who was going out with whom. Although he hadn't seen Emma with other girls he felt sure that she didn't giggle and she obviously didn't spend a lot of time on her hair or makeup.

Callum thought all of this as they pulled into the bay in Iain's boat. The sand shelved steeply and the tide was coming in so it was easy for Callum to run the boat into the sand and let Emma out. As she jumped and landed on the pure white sand of the completely deserted beach three miles across bogs from anywhere, Callum gunned the engine in reverse and pulled away from the beach. "I'll see you back at Fionnphort!" he shouted in glee. This was a joke that Iain had played on him, and countless drivers of boats and cars had played on people for hundreds of years. Emma was supposed to be overcome with the fear of being left behind. Callum could then turn the boat, race back into the shore and shout "only joking!"

But she didn't shout. She didn't react at all. She just stood there looking confused, and sad.

Callum turned the boat and landed. He threw out the anchor and jumped on to the beach. Emma was just looking at him.

"I wasne going to leave ye know" said Callum.

"Why did you pretend? I don't like pretend like that. I believe you and that makes me sad."

"Sorry," said Callum.

One minute he was thinking how much he liked Emma and the next she goes and does something like that. It was only a joke! Come to think of it he hadn't seen Emma laugh except the once. She was a seriously serious person.

"Do you ever laugh?" he asked, with a hint of accusation in his voice.

"Sometimes," Emma replied.

For five or six minutes Callum and Emma were lost in their own thoughts gazing out to sea and then Emma asked: "what's it like when you teletransfer?"

Callum knew that this question would be asked by

someone at sometime, and he had been rehearsing the first part of his answer.

"You know when you taste something new? How can you describe what it tastes like? Last year my mum and dad took me to the Indian restaurant in Tobermory and I had a curry. What did it taste like? I can't describe it because it was new. If you've had a curry, I can say that it tastes like a curry and you will understand. It's a bit like that with teletransfering. The first time I did it, it made me feel really sick and it felt a bit like it does when you spin round and round and round while looking straight up…not quite like that though because you haven't moved. It is much easier now and quicker, now I know what is happening. Does that make sense?"

"A bit," said Emma hesitantly. "Is there any animal you can't teletransfer into?"

"I don't know, I've only done the buzzard, the rabbit, the gull twice, an oyster catcher and the seal."

"I think you've done more than that," said Emma enigmatically.

"What do you mean?" demanded Callum.

"Do you think you could do an insect?"

"I'm not sure, I could try."

"Try this sand flea then."

"Only if you catch it and look after it. What if I can't transfer back?"

Emma shrugged, "you won't know if you don't try."

"Thanks a lot for all your concern!" said Callum already preparing for his transfer. This all still felt very new and he wasn't sure if he wanted to be a bug. Oh well, give it a try.

Callum looked at the sand flea, a small hopping crustacean which looked like a very small prawn that lives in sand and jumps a lot, and he wondered what it would be like to be one.

He wondered much harder what it would be like to be one.

Even harder.

"What's happening?" asked Emma.

"Nothing," said Callum.

"Are you doing it right?"

"How do I know? I've only ever done it four times and I've only been able to do it for three days. I'm still not convinced that this isn't a really realistic and graphic dream. Perhaps I can't do it anymore." As Callum said this he couldn't decide whether or not this would be a good thing. During the last few days he had begun to wonder if there might not be some responsibility for being able to teletransfer. Maybe it wasn't all flying around playing tricks on people, listening to conversations, and peeking through windows as he had previously imagined. Maybe with great power there really was great responsibility, just like in Spiderman.

"Have a go at that rabbit over there," said Emma, "see if you can still do it."

"OK," said Callum "but I have a bad history with being in a rabbit, don't forget I got eaten last time."

Callum focussed on the rabbit this time and felt the now familiar dizziness and nausea, his vision cleared and he was able to look back at himself and Emma. As he expected, he was lying down next to Emma who was sitting up.

Hold on, Emma was leaning down to his now supine body. What was she doing? Was she kissing him? Aaargh! He wasn't even there! Without thinking, he was hopping as fast as he could across the grass and across the sand towards her. She looked up and he could see that she was laughing now. Head back, eyes sparkling, teeth shining, guffawing laughing. He got there and shouted; "Shut up! What were you doing to my body? Why are you laughing?"

Through her laughter with tears running down her face now, she replied, "I can't understand you, you know. You're a rabbit! You're just making squeaking noises!"

Callum concentrated on himself and was quickly sitting up and frowning at Emma.

"I'm sure it was very funny! Now what were you doing to my body? You kissed me!" shouted Callum.

"I whispered to you," said Emma who had stopped laughing now.

"You what?"

"I whispered. I wanted to know if you would hear me. Why would I want to kiss you?"

"Errmm…it looked like you were kissing me from over there." Callum blushed and turned and pointed to where he had been in the rabbit, just in time to see the rabbit dive down its burrow, presumably disturbed by it suddenly finding itself in the middle of a beach and very exposed.

"I wanted to know exactly what you are able to do and what you aren't able to do," Emma interrupted Callum's thoughts.

"Can you move your body when you are in another animal? Can you hear me if I talk to you? Can you talk to me when you are in another animal? There are loads of questions about your new talent that you need to know the answers to."

"Why?" asked Callum. "Why do I need to know? What are you not telling me? What have you found out?"

"Nothing certain."

"I thought you never lied!" shouted Callum.

"You've asked me, so I will tell you, but you should prepare yourself for a shock. There was one other case of someone claiming to be able to do what you can do. It was in France two years ago. She was 12 just like you and within two weeks she had disappeared. She lived in a remote part of Brittany and before she could do a proper scientific test to prove she could teletransfer, she had disappeared. Her body was found, chewed by what the forensic team thought was a great white shark."

"So what has this got to do with me?" demanded Callum.

"The French police suspected foul play. I think you should find out all you can about what you can do and be prepared to defend yourself."

"You're mad. This is Fionnphort on Mull on the west coast of Scotland. I've told no one but you. How would anything happen to me?"

The rest of the afternoon was spent lying on the beach and chatting about nothing much. At one point Emma fell asleep and Callum couldn't resist transferring into a sheep and bleating in her ear to wake her up. Emma wasn't convinced that that was funny either. So squeaking rabbits were hilarious but bleating sheep not so much...

While they were chatting, Callum began to reflect on what Emma had said. Maybe he did need to practise the transferring thing and find out exactly what he could and couldn't do. It couldn't hurt. He would be able to find out anything, go anywhere. See things that no one else had seen, do things that no one else had done. It would be really cool. He grinned thinking about all the mischief he could get up to.

They left in plenty of time to get back home in time for tea and Callum had a go at teletransfering into a gannet and a puffin. Both went well but he felt nothing new. No new skills or abilities and his body just lay there, on the one occasion dribbling slightly. What he did learn was that four transfers in only a few hours had left him drained and exhausted.

When they landed they walked up from the quay; past the tourists getting back from Iona, past the lorry that came all the way from Spain to collect the shellfish that the local fishermen caught, past the shop where they saw Mrs McDougall gossiping to the long-suffering Morag, and past the cemetery to the ferryman's cottages. It was when they passed the Crossing Shop that Callum started to think of the reality of what was about to happen. He was taking his first girl friend (although not girlfriend), home for tea. His mum would be trying too hard to make Emma feel comfortable, his dad would take every opportunity to tease him. Emma would say something 'honest' and it could be an unmitigated nightmare. The feelings that he was beginning to have in his stomach were described by others as 'butterflies'. Butterflies! Callum thought something larger would be more appropriate, bats maybe, or vultures.

They walked through the front door and all of Callum's worst nightmares began unfolding. First there was the smell. Bleach combined with air freshener, fish, furniture polish and tobacco smoke. Oh no. This meant that Mrs McBride had gone the whole hog to make Emma feel welcome. She had turned a really pleasant family cottage into a sterilised hospital wing. Everything had been cleaned, tidied and scrubbed. Mr McBride (who only ever smoked when his wife started cleaning manically), was sitting in his chair which had been moved from its normal position in front of the TV, to in front of the window where his craggy dark face was in deep shadow.

"Mum, Dad, this is Emma. Emma this is my mum and dad."

"Och it's lovely to meet ye, ye've turned his wee head lass, I think he's fallen for ye!" said Callum's mum embarrassingly.

"Aye" said Callum's dad, although what he was agreeing to wasn't particularly clear to anyone.

"Hello," said Emma. "Did you know that there are over three hundred chemicals in tobacco and over half of them are carcinogenic?"

"Aye, I did, and did you know that ye have very short hair for a girl?" grunted Mr McBride with a deep gravely disapproval.

"Yes I do," said Emma, "but it is much easier to look after and I don't care what other people think."

It's not the start I hoped for but at least it can't get any worse thought Callum.

"Why does the house smell of fish?" asked Emma.

Really? Really? "Why does the house smell of fish?" and just when he thought it couldn't get any worse!

Mrs McBride scowled at Callum now having obviously discarded any intention to make this experience painless for him.

"Tha' wud be the fish dear, but don't ye worry aboot that. Y'll get used te it. Anyway I've got a whole set of babby photie's for ye to look at afore ye go!" pronounced Mrs McBride.

Mr McBride grunted with humorous approval and they both scowled at both Emma and Callum. Luckily Emma didn't seem to notice so it was only the three of them that sat through dinner steaming at each other.

"Have ye kissed her yet then?" was Mr McBride's offering with a wry grin on his face.

"No. Callum hasn't kissed me yet," said Emma, "although he accused me of trying to kiss him this afternoon."

"Aye, that'd be the wishful thinking," said Mr McBride warming to Emma.

"Do ye expect him to kiss ye then?" asked Mrs McBride with a huge grin on her face, obviously enjoying Callum's discomfiture as much as Mr McBride.

"I don't know," mused Emma. "We have only known each other for a few days and I don't know if he likes me like that. I can never tell if people like me at all, let alone like that."

Callum was scarlet with embarrassment and was slowly sinking below the table. His mum and dad were enjoying themselves enormously. The only saving grace was that they had seemed to get over their annoyance with Emma.

Callum was pleased that Emma was no longer annoying them, right up to the point where she turned to him and asked "Do you like me like that Callum?"

What was he supposed to say to that? The conversation had been poking fun at him, laughing at him being embarrassed in a good-natured way. This was now a serious question. Both his mum and dad stopped smiling and looked away from the table. They couldn't help him now. That was not a question to ask in public let alone in front of his mum and dad. Why had Emma gone and asked a question like that? Callum knew that he ran the risk of offending Emma or getting himself more involved than he wanted to be.

"No," said Callum quietly. "I don't like you like that. I'm only 12 and I've only known you a few days." He had decided to take a leaf out of Emma's book and play it straight. Even as he spoke he could hear his mother's sharp intake of breath, and the tension was palpable. All three McBrides waited for Emma's reply with breath that was truly bated.

"Good," said Emma.

Callum could hear the breath being released by his mum and dad. It sounded remarkably like the hiss of air as he opened the breather hole on the petrol tank on Iain's boat.

The rest of the meal went well with the occasional awkward moment that Callum was able to fill, but the time came when Emma was due to leave.

"Thank you very much for tea Mrs McBride." Emma dutifully said. "It was lovely, except the fish. I don't like fish much."

As Mr McBride led Emma to the door, Mrs McBride hissed to Callum, "Ye were right Cal, a right weird one, but nice wi'it! Ye've nay done badly lad. Now walk her home."

"So what do you think of them?" asked Callum as they walked up the hill past the cemetery.

"I think they are very nice," said Emma, "although I can't understand everything that your mum says, and your dad is a bit scary."

"They liked you," said Callum.

A few moments passed before Emma answered; "I'm pleased," she said. Callum took this to be a good sign and they walked on in silence.

The time was about 10.30 pm and the sunset over the island was a fireburst of colour, the oranges and reds staining the undersides of the cirrus cloud boded well for the weather tomorrow. Maybe he would try and kiss Emma. You never know it might not be too bad and it would give him something exciting that he could e-mail to Andrew.

"Did you know that sunsets have been getting more and more vivid over the last 100 years?" asked Emma. "It's because the increasing levels of pollution help to reflect the light."

That was romantic thought Callum. Maybe I won't bother. The conversation stayed on the pollution lines with Emma revealing that she knew an awful lot about the chemistry involved until they were in sight of her house.

"...so the chlorofluorocarbons that were released five years ago will take another fifteen..."

"Shhhh!" Callum interrupted. "Your front door is bust!"

"What?"

"Your front door is broken! Look."

The two of them ran to the house and pushed the door open. Whatever had happened hadn't been a gentle affair. The front room was completely destroyed. It looked as if a forklift truck had gone berserk. The TV was smashed in one corner, the couch was up-ended and even the carpet had been ripped along with the curtains.

"MUM! DAD! WHERE ARE YOU?" Emma ran from room to room shouting. All the rooms were trashed except for her own. Emma's room, the only room upstairs, was like an island of calm in a stormy sea.

"Where are they?" Emma asked Callum plaintively. The confident girl that Callum had known until a moment before was beginning to dissolve into tears.

"Maybe they were out?" said Callum, not really believing it himself. He knew that they had been waiting in for Emma to return, no doubt to interrogate her about her new friend's family.

"Where are they?" Emma asked again sinking to her knees and starting to sob huge wracking sobs that shook her entire body.

Callum knew when he was out of his depth. He needed Mrs McBride and he needed her now.

"Come on Emma," said Callum. "We need to tell the police and you need to be somewhere else. Don't worry your mum and dad will turn up."

At hearing Callum's soothing, reassuring words, Emma slowly stood turned to Callum and screamed in his face;

"This is your fault! You and your 'skill' have got my parents killed. They were taken because of YOU!"

Callum took Emma's hand and started to walk quickly back to his parents. He didn't know why she had shouted at him, he just knew that Emma needed Mrs McBride.

He also thought that it wouldn't be a good time to tell Emma that she had what looked like blood soaked into the knees of her trousers, although he wasn't sure if there ever would be a good time.

Chapter 4

Wednesday Afternoon Carl

"Doctor, why are we going back to Iona so soon?"

"I have received information that there may be another who possesses your ability to teletransfer. I have been keeping an eye on him for several years and I thought that he did not have the ability. It is time to tell you that you have a brother, an identical twin. When you were both born, you were the eldest and you showed all the signs of having the ability to teletransfer and your brother did not. I chose you, therefore, to be my protégé and heir. The other child I allowed to be adopted by some local ferryman. As you know I was fond of your wayward mother."

Doctor Slack was a tall man with a soft lilting Welsh accent giving away his Cardiff upbringing. He was largely unremarkable with brown eyes and brown hair. The sort of person that you could pass on the street without ever noticing that you had. That was until you looked into his eyes. They say that the eyes are windows to the soul and if that were true then Doctor Slack didn't have a soul. His eyes were empty and dead, brown in colour but dull steel in lustre.

"There was a remarkable rescue yesterday of a small child by a dolphin. It all sounded too implausible not to be the work of a teletransferer. My spy in the village did some investigating and this other boy, 'Callum', your twin, was present at the rescue. I assume therefore that it was him, and that he is also a teletransferer. It was always a possibility."

"Will he have to 'disappear' Doctor? It would be a shame if that were to happen before I could test myself against him. After all, I beat that French girl."

"Calm yourself Carl. I will see to it that you continue to develop your skills and get tested along the way. After all, we have the ultimate prize to aim for… Now we have a few hours cruise before we get to Iona so I would like you to practice extending your transfer time. It is just a matter of stamina, I am sure."

"Certainly Doctor" said Carl.

"Oh Carl!" shouted the Doctor after him.

"Yes Doctor?"

"Are you not curious about this brother of yours?"

"Should I be Doctor? I have never met him. I am only interested in whether he can help us towards our goal. Just because we share DNA and a skill that he has picked up rather later in life, why should I care about him…more than…" Carl searched around for something to compare Callum to and saw a beetle crawling on the deck "…this beetle for example?" Carl stepped forward and deliberately crushed the beetle underfoot.

Slack laughed in a cold and humourless way. "Good boy, Carl. Sometimes you surprise even me! Get on with your training."

Carl made his way down the steps into the stateroom of the twenty-metre luxury cruiser that was currently powering its way along the Sound of Mull. It was a beautiful streamlined craft that had cost Slack nearly three million pounds. It was equipped with dual inboard Mercruisers and had been completely refitted to provide everything they needed including the staff of 4. It had set off barely an hour ago from where it was moored just south of Oban in the grounds of the luxury house that Doctor Christian Slack had built eleven years ago, paying for everything in cash. Carl didn't know where the money had come from, or where it was still coming from. The Doctor had assured him that he needn't worry about little things like that. All he had to do was prepare himself for the task ahead. The Doctor provided private tutors in their Mayfair apartment in London and spoke with him every day. He was equipped with everything he needed. He was a black belt in Jujitsu (one of the youngest in the country) and had already taken all of his GCSE's with straight 9's and was currently working on his 'A' Levels. His specialism was pharmacology, like the Doctor, with an emphasis on the genetic mutations that could occur with excessive drug taking. It was him who had been monitoring search terms that had been entered into the more common internet search engines, and it was him who had found that there had been a lot of interest from the computer of a Professor Higgins in Fionnphort.

The Doctor had been most interested.

Yes, Carl's life was that of a very wealthy celebrity, but without the inconvenience of actually being a celebrity. He spent large periods of time on his own but was given everything he needed to succeed, and hadn't the Doctor always told him that he was better than other children? Why would he need to mix with inferiors? The Doctor had explained that he really didn't need friends. Friends and family were a source of weakness and were to be spurned at every opportunity.

Through the stateroom and past the bathroom and the galley, but before the sleeping quarters, was his practice room. If the Doctor and he were to succeed in achieving their goal then he would need to be able to spend a long time in a transfer, and as he had found out on numerous occasions the longer he spent in a transfer the more chance there was that his life force would slip away, stretched between his body and the animal that he transferred into. His sense of self, slowly getting less and less and his body getting weaker and weaker.

Carl entered the practice room and was greeted by the usual shriek and growl and splash of its inhabitants. This room was recreated in each of the places that Carl lived. The walls were filled with tanks, and cages with an assortment of the sorts of animals that might be found around this part of the world. There was even a golden eagle in a cage so small that it couldn't even open its wings. In fact

Carl knew that this particular eagle, now two years old had never opened its wings. Two of the Doctor's employees had risked imprisonment when they had stolen the unhatched egg from a very tall pine tree in Mull. The eagle was needed for its eyesight, its endurance and its carrying ability. Behind Carl was a dentist's reclining chair with an array of medical instrumentation placed behind. Carl relaxed onto the chair, attached electrodes to his own head, and put on a wrist band. Instantly the instruments behind him started up with information about his heart rate, his breathing rate and depth, and his brain activity displayed on bright colourful screens. As soon as he was comfortable he focussed all his might on the smallest cage. An insignificant cage on the floor nearest the door. In this cage was a cockroach; a fat healthy scurrying cockroach. Again it didn't work. He was close, he could feel that he was nearly going in, nearly teletransferring into an insect. Something that, as far as he knew, no one else had ever done. It was crucial to the plan, that he should be able to do it.

He did as the Doctor had told him and moved on to his endurance testing. The Doctor had explained very early in his training that when he transferred, he left his body with very little life force.

Carl mused on the concept of 'life force', science had answered a lot of the great questions…but there were a few outstanding. What, for example is 'gravity'? Science can describe its effects and can come up with an equation to describe those effects, but no one can tell you what it is. Gravity is described as the force between two masses that is proportional to the product of their masses and inversely proportional to the square of the distance between, them but what is it? What is that force? What is gravity? No one can tell you. Carl had had fun with a tutor once with that one. Of course, the biggest question still left to science is 'what is life?' Carl's tutors had taught him that for a 'thing' to be characterised as 'alive' it must have several attributes, it must respire, reproduce etc. …but what IS life? What is it that makes a pile of cells (a human body) alive one second and then not the next? Carl certainly didn't know and nor did anyone else, what he was keen on was that his particular pile of cells stayed alive for as long as was possible.

The longer he was away from his body, the more that little bit of life force that was left behind in his body ebbed away. If he was away from his body for too long, then his body could die. If that happened he could either be left inside the animal that he was last in, or more probably, he would die as well.

No one knew…and if he was left inside the body of a small rodent for example, who would ever know?

What the Doctor did know was that after about an hour away from your own body, it would die. The Doctor knew this from the tests that were done for the government in the 90s on unsuspecting servicemen. Several must have died for the Doctor to get this information. So if his body died, would he? He didn't want to find out which was why he had been trying to extend his time in a transfer for months.

So far, Carl had pushed this up to 80 minutes. He would transfer into an animal and then watch his own body signs on the monitors until it seemed that his body was dying, then he would transfer back. As the Doctor had predicted this seemed to train his body into lasting longer when he was away in another creature.

This time Carl chose an otter. He liked the way its mind worked when he opened it. He liked the way that it was always optimistic. He liked the way that it killed its prey with a laugh in its mind. Otters were common where he would be proving himself to the Doctor and achieving their goal.

As usual, there were the beginnings of nausea and disorientation, but he was very fast at being the otter now. He checked that he could see the monitors and then the bit that he liked best. He could get the otter to do what he wanted just by willing it to, but by opening its mind he could overpower it. He could dominate the animal completely, he could manipulate its emotions and control every aspect of its being. He could make it afraid, he could make it happy, he could make it hungry, and he could make it despair. Once, when he had been honing his skills, he occupied the mind of a shrew. He did not know how delicate it was and when he scared its simple mammal mind, he overdid it slightly and the animal died. No one knew what would happen if an animal died until then, when he had simply returned to his own body. The Doctor had been cross with the waste of the shrew's life and now he was careful when he enjoyed the terror of a small creature, not to let it die. It was becoming an art form. Pushing the animal until its fear was so much that its heart was being stimulated by the adrenaline to the point of bursting, and then backing off. He felt a rush of power that was even more thrilling than flying or being a dolphin.

This time he was concentrating on extending his transfer time, so he left the animal to do what it wanted in its tiny cage, while he stayed on as a passenger watching the monitors.

After about an hour he could see the Doctor enter the room.

"Carl, don't come back, carry on with your training. Are you in the otter? As usual. I would like you to vary your transfers in future. Anyway, I have come to ask you if you have a list of sites that the good Professor Higgins visited while he was searching about us. We will be asking him some questions when we arrive shortly."

From the otter, Carl could watch his body as with enormous effort he half transferred back and nodded. The Doctor did not expect it to be a necessary skill for their goal to be achieved but it was useful on occasions like this. Carl wasn't sure that the Doctor fully realised the effort that it took him, even though he had explained it. It took the same amount of effort as if he had completely transferred into his body and back again. It also meant that he lost some of his control of the animal. It didn't matter today because he was just a passenger and also the Doctor did not require speech today.

"Good Carl. Is it on a file on the desktop?"

Carl's body nodded again.

"I will not keep you. I know how you say that it tires you." said the Doctor as he left the room.

Carl was very pleased when he finally gave up and jumped back into his body. It was just in time, his heart rate was down to 38 beats per minute and his breathing had practically stopped, but he had pushed it to 86 minutes. The Doctor would be pleased.

The Doctor was always pleased with his Carl.

Ever since Doctor Christian Slack had headed the team that had experimented on the soldiers in the 90s, he had been taken with the possibilities that it provided. In return for his silence about the morality of the tests he had been encouraged to administer by his military bosses, he had been given the secret LSD manufacturing plant on Iona when the government had pulled out. Using a religious cult as cover, he had been able to increase the output and make a considerable amount of money with a small cut going back to the people in the MoD who had originally employed him to do the testing, it had proven a highly lucrative enterprise. With nobody looking at a religious group full of decidedly odd people, he had been able to set up a pan-European distribution via yachts and the shellfish that were routinely driven from Fionnphort to their markets in Spain and Portugal. From there, the drugs could be shipped around Europe. Even more important had been that the religious cover group had been very successful in recruiting waifs and strays, who in turn had been very good subjects for his continued experimentation. It was a shame that so many of them had to die and be disposed of in the waters of the North Atlantic. It was a good job that the sea was so full of carnivores.

It looked like the sea would have to take a few more. Professor Higgins and his wife would have to learn that nosing through the internet wasn't always 'safe surfing', and after the Higgins he would have to consider the future of Callum McBride.

He was actually very pleased that Callum had developed the ability to teletransfer. It would give him a backup if Carl were to underperform in the task he had set for him. In the task, which when successful, would set him up with enough money to buy a small country. Enough money to be above the petty laws that held him back, that meant that he had to restrict his experiments that could make man far greater, that could make man achieve the greatness that was there in his DNA. His drugs could push evolution beyond the dreams of most scientists.

Slack thought about Carl. He had been very fond of Carl's mother. She was a wild and crazy thing in her early 20s when she had first been brought to Iona looking for some sort of spiritual salvation. Instead she had found him and he supplied her with the drugs she craved to escape her own reality. When she discovered she was pregnant with twins she wanted to leave…tried to leave, but he couldn't allow that. So, when they were born he chose the eldest, the one with the eyes that reminded him of his own and decided to carry on his experimentation and see if what he had dreamt of was possible. It had turned out that it was possible and Carl could transfer at will into most animals. Carl had never taken LSD as far as Slack was aware and was the living embodiment of his own brilliance! The only shame was that he had not managed to duplicate, to repeat his experiment. In science when you have done something brilliant it is always good to do it again before you show it to the world and now with this 'Callum' he had two of them. Besides, if anything happened to Carl he would need to replace him and Callum would be ideal. Obviously he would miss Carl but like everything else in his life ultimately Carl was replaceable.

As he was musing, he felt a vibration on his side. He picked up his mobile and checked the number. It was his man in Fionnphort, there must be news.

"Slack." he barked into the phone

"Doctor, we've got the professor and his wife. He put up a bigger struggle than we thought, and there is some other news."

The Doctor could tell from the tone of the voice that the news would not be good. "What news?"

"There is a daughter. She was out at the time."

"Did you see her room. Does she have a PC?" demanded the Doctor.

"We didn't know she existed until after we got out. Her room must have been in the roof space."

"Damn! It could have been her! If they have a small network we wouldn't know from the outside whose computer it was, they will share an IP address."

"And Doctor, there is more. She was out...at the house of Callum McBride!"

"What do I pay you for? Idiot! You will have to dispose of the parents and get her another time. Now we will have to deal with police all over the place. Still they are idiots...LIKE YOU!" The Doctor shut the phone and sat down looking thoughtful. He may have to move faster in the matter of Callum McBride than he would have liked.

Chapter 5

Wednesday Night Callum

Callum quickly led Emma back to his own house. Emma had gone very quiet and was stumbling along. Callum had seen something like it last year when a family, who had been out in a sailboat, had been rescued after three days. They had been blown onto an uninhabited island where their boat was holed. They didn't have a radio or a flare, or any appropriate safety equipment, and it had taken the Coastguard two days to be told that they were missing (when they didn't come back to the campsite), and another day to find them. It always amazed people how difficult it was for the coastguard to find people who disappeared off the coast. What they didn't realise was that there were hundreds of islands all with caves and beaches, a coastline that is thousands of miles long. Callum had been there when they were led up the slipway with the same vacant expression on their faces as Emma had on hers now. Mrs McBride had been there to look after them. "It's shock Cal. Ye have te reassure them and keep them warm."

"Emma, it's going to be fine. The police will find them. They probably went for a walk or something."

Emma said nothing but began to sob again. Great silent wracking sobs, like the rise of a swell and the breaking of a wave.

Mrs McBride was incredulous when Callum told her what they had found when they went back to Emma's house, but she clicked into nurse mode and took Emma into the kitchen murmuring in her ear. Mr McBride moved faster than Callum had ever seen. He rang the local police...Angus Green; a tall, bicycling, laid-back, character who Callum had known his whole life. Angus was a great local copper but did he have the experience to be able to cope with...cope with what? Kidnapping? Murder?

Callum went into the kitchen to see how Emma was coping only to be shushed out by Mrs McBride. "Callum, I'm putting young wee Emma to bed in Isla's room. She's no to be bothered 'til the morning. She's had a terrible shock and she needs te sleep! Ye get off te bed and we'll see what's happenin' in the mornin'."

So Callum did what he was told and went upstairs to lie on his bed. As he lay down, Emma's words came back to him; "This is your fault! You and your 'skill' have got my parents killed. They were taken because of YOU!"

What if Emma was right? Who could he tell what he could do? Who would believe him? There was no one here he could tell so they might not think that someone else was involved. Why were they taken? They couldn't be of any use to anyone, could they?

Callum could remember loads of TV announcements describing similar scenes when the husband had gone berserk and killed his wife. They were usually followed up by a report the following day that the husband had been found dead in his car full of exhaust gases. He could hear Angus arrive, which he thought was both quick and a bit odd as he would have expected him to have gone straight to the scene. He could hear voices but not the words. As he had done countless times before Callum climbed out of his window and slipped silently down the drainpipe until he was crouched outside his own front window that was slightly open in the warm July evening.

"They'll turn up deed, I'm telling ye," pronounced PC Green.

"Keep yer voice doon Angus, the wee gerl is just above yon heed there," whispered Mrs McBride.

"Should ye not be up at the hoose there Angus?" was Mr McBride's gravelly voice.

"No. I was in the pub when I got ye call there, so I popped over in the van wi the tape an I've taped it all up. I'm no allowed in 'til the squad come over tomorrow to do all the forensic stuff an all. There's nowt to do now but wait here. Aye I will, thank ye, another wee dram would go doon nicely."

Callum's eavesdropping was interrupted by a rustling noise and a wet snout being thrust into his face. He jumped a mile and was about to yell, when he recognised Lottie, his neighbour's dog. She was doing her usual nightly round of the local properties before she went to bed to dream of chasing rabbits. Callum was a bit more sympathetic to the rabbits' cause than he had been a few nights previously after his experience with the buzzard on the top of the hill only two days before.

Was it only two days? It felt like weeks!

Having heard everything useful that he expected to, he climbed back up the drainpipe with the help of the shed, and in through his open window.

So nobody was going to do anything to help until tomorrow.

It could be too late by then!

Emma had scared him when she'd told him about the French girl. Perhaps this was all his fault.

Just as he was lapsing into despair, a thought struck him. Maybe there wasn't a lot a 12 year old boy could do but Lottie was a four year old labradoodle (a cross between a labrador and a poodle), with a nose that could sniff out anything. Callum immediately looked out of the window and scanned for Lottie, not easy as she was a dark ginger in colour. As usual she had wandered on to the beach for her last sniff of the evening. Callum reasoned that if he could teletransfer into Lottie he might be able to pick up a scent and then in the morning he could find a way to lead the police to rescue Emma's parents if they weren't dead already. The problem was he was in his room. Last time he had transferred into an animal and lost sight of his body he had snapped back into it. If he stayed in his room, he would be out of sight immediately and would get nowhere. There was nothing else for it. He climbed back down the drainpipe and picked his way carefully through the vegetable patch and over the fence out onto the beach.

"Come on Lottie!" he urged as he walked purposefully to the huge boulder in the middle of the beach. The boulder was an erratic, dropped by the ice when it retreated at the end of the last ice age 12,000 years ago. At one point it had been drilled by the miners of the famed Fionnphort red granite that could be found in such illustrious places as Blackfriars Bridge, Holborn Viaduct and The Albert Memorial in London and as far away as the New York Docks, but before it could be cut up and carted away the local Lord banned the work and the rock stayed where it is today.

Using the split in the boulder, Callum scrambled up to the top of the rock while Lottie looked on interestedly. He lay down so that he wouldn't roll off. From here he could see most of the village, but more importantly, he was visible to anyone or any dog, that looked.

Callum then wondered what it would be like to be Lottie. He found that he didn't need to actually wonder, he just focussed on being Lottie and he transferred. Every time he did it, it was quicker, and he felt less nauseous. As soon as he was in Lottie, he ran flat out up to Emma's house and again was shocked by the violence of the scene. PC Green had obviously tried to shut the door as best he could but it wasn't going to close without the help of a joiner.

So now all he needed to do was pick up a scent and follow it. Callum made Lottie put her nose to the floor and sniff, in the same way that he could make his own hand in his own body wave. He could even smell the odours that came back. They were clearer than when he was in his own body, but he couldn't interpret them. Of course! How stupid. He could make Lottie go to the house and sniff, but he didn't know how to identify or follow a scent. Now what? Every transfer was an effort and it looked like this one had been wasted.

While he was mulling over this problem and trying to work out what each of the smells might be heard himself ask his canine friend absentmindedly. "What do you think Lottie?"

As he asked Callum felt something pushing on his consciousness, something was pushing to get in. He thought that it felt a bit like a memory. It felt like when you really knew that you knew something and it was just on the tip of your tongue, but you couldn't quite get it to the forefront of your mind.

Callum reached for it with his mind in the same way that you might concentrate to reach a memory, a forgotten telephone number, or a name, or where you put your dad's car keys, and then it happened. Like a kaleidoscope of emotions, Callum felt 'Lottie' wash all over him. He had found the 'Lottie' from within. Lottie was curious, Lottie was happy to be out smelling the smells, Lottie was interested in Callum being in her head, but not scared. Lottie was up for anything. Lottie was a dog.

This was what it was like to be a dog, and it was incredible! Lottie was happy. Not just 'thanks for lending me the boat Iain' happy, but deep deep down happy. Lottie KNEW that everything was going to be OK. Everything was a game and would end up fine. The confidence flowed through Callum's consciousness so Callum hesitantly asked Lottie to pick up the scent of blood and follow it. You never know, with Lottie's overwhelming positivity it might work?

Amazingly Lottie seemed to understand. It wasn't by language, it was as if they were the same creature, but Callum was in control. Lottie put her nose to the blood on the carpet and then started to quarter the pavement and the road outside the house. Callum had seen trained sheepdogs do this but never Lottie. So she did know how, she just couldn't normally be bothered!

Within seconds Lottie had picked up the scent. Although Callum could smell all the same smells he couldn't distinguish between them but Lottie could. She was off like a flash back down the lane to the road into the village where she turned right. So they didn't take them out by boat from Fionnphort then, thought Callum. At this point Callum realised that they had been following a trail of very fine droplets and after about 50 metres they disappeared. Lottie started quartering again, at first in front and then behind. Callum surmised that they had been in a car and had accelerated at this point so the spaces between the droplets would be getting bigger and bigger. "Forward Lottie" Callum urged. We need to go forward and we can find the next droplet. Lottie walked slowly forward with her snout to the ground. Sure enough, about ten metres in front Lottie found another droplet and ten metres in front another. Callum was amazed at his luck so far and how well his plan was working.

"Run now Lottie, let's see where they are going!" So, on they ran, Callum thrilled by his success and Lottie having a great evening, albeit mindful of the telling off she would get when she finally got home. Still everything would be fine…she was a dog after all and everything will always be fine.

About a quarter of a mile outside the village, Lottie pulled up short with her snout to the ground and turned to follow a track off to the left. Callum made Lottie stop. The track only led to three houses and the old quay in Bull Hole where they used to load the granite from the old quarry. Now he knew that they must have taken the Higgins down to the quay and loaded them on to a boat. The tide was perfect. If they had kidnapped them and waited for all the fishing, yachting and ferry traffic to stop they would have had to wait until about 10.30 pm when all the yachtspeople took their dinghy's back to their moorings having eaten in the only restaurant in Fionnphort (it was attached to the only pub). It was 11.30 pm now so they could only have an hour's head start wherever they were going. If they were in a fast cruiser or a RIB he was sunk, but if they were in a fishing boat, then he still had a chance. He couldn't follow in Lottie he would have to go back to his body and find a better animal to follow with…his body, he couldn't see his body…he couldn't sense his body.

As soon as this realisation hit him he could feel himself being stretched like elastic and just as he felt like he might break, he was back in his body, sitting on the rock in the middle of Fionnphort bay, leaving poor old Lottie out on the Craignure road.

Maybe it wasn't about seeing his body, more about being able to sense it thought Callum.

"Thanks Lottie!" Callum whispered into the night.

Callum was both hopeful and despondent. He knew where they were being taken to and there was a chance he could follow them, but he needed a night animal that could see in the dark and be quick. A bird would be best. An owl wouldn't like it over water but would have the best night vision and Callum didn't know how far they intended to take the Higgins. They might have just motored around the headland, if they had taken them to the quay at all! Perhaps they had just taken them to the quarry to murder them. It would be a good, quiet place. Whatever had happened he needed to get high and high with great vision.

Just then Callum heard what he had been hoping for. The quiet hoot of a male tawny owl somewhere back towards Lottie. "Twit" "Twit". Callum waited for the "Twoo" but it didn't come. People often thought that tawny owls made a "Twit Twoo" call but that is actually the male calling and the female answering so what Callum could hear was a male tawny calling for a mate.

Come on! Thought Callum, I can't see you! He looked towards where he thought the owl would be and focussed.

It worked. Even without seeing the owl, he knew it was there and that seemed to be enough. He found himself in a tawny owl flying higher and higher, at 50 metres he could see the quarry, and amazingly everything in it. His vision was like an old style black and white TV. Grayscale the computer people called it, but with a resolution a human could only dream of. There was nothing there. At

100 metres he could see all of Fionnphort, Iona and out to the surrounding islands, but he could see no boat. He flew quickly towards the old quarry quayside and began to doubt his theory. Nothing. Fly closer and YES! There it was! A boat trail on the surface! That had to be it! When a boat disturbs the surface of the water you can often see the trace of where it has been, a trail laid out for him to follow. If no other boats cross or disturb it, and if the wind isn't too strong to cause the waves to crest, he should be able to follow it all the way to the Higgins!

Now let's see how fast this owl can fly!

Callum pointed the owl along Bull Hole following the trail inadvertently laid in the water by whoever had taken the Higgins. As he was flying parallel to the coast and only a few metres from it the owl did a fantastic job, but as soon as he turned out to sea, he could feel enormous pressure on his mind, just like with Lottie. Again he searched with his mind for the owl and as he joined with it he could feel its fear. It wanted to turn back, it hated the water, it needed to turn back, this was not its choice, get away from the water, fly inland. The fear was almost overwhelming but Callum found he could easily force the owl to comply. Further and further he pushed the owl, until he felt the stretching. His body was still laid out on the rock in the bay and he had left it too far behind. He calmed the owl and pointed it back towards land and safety and let himself spring back to his body.

When he came to himself on the rock, he came to a dawning realisation. If he was going to follow the Higgins then so was his body. He would take Iain's boat. It would be more difficult by sea but he already knew which way they were heading, which was towards Staffa, the tourist island. If he could gain on them then he could...he could what? Transfer into an animal while his boat motored on into oblivion? If his body was going to go it would need someone to look after it. But who?

Callum knew he had no choice. No one else would believe him. No one else would be ready to risk it. He didn't want to get her into any more danger, but he had to ask her. No one else would dream of following him into the North Atlantic in a 4 m boat with a single, tiny engine.

Callum jumped from the rock and ran home. He was feeling it now. It had already been a long tiring day and all these transfers were taking it out of him but time was now, very much of the essence. That boat trail wouldn't last forever. He got back into his room and, checking that the adults were still downstairs, he sneaked into Isla's bedroom. The room was pitch black with the door closed but Callum didn't want to risk putting the light on. He felt his way over to the bed and ran his hands over it, looking for Emma.

"What do you want?"

Emma's voice came from the chair in the corner of the room and it made Callum jump several centimetres. He could feel his skin crawl with the adrenaline.

"I want your help to find your parents."

"Haven't you done enough?" asked Emma.

"Emma, I havne done anything. I'm just me."

"Because of you, my parents are gone, probably dead," said Emma. As Callum's eyes adjusted, he could see her dark eyes glowing in the faint light from the window.

"Aye, maybe so, but it wasne my doing. I've found their trail. With your help we may be able to find them in time, but I can't do it on my own. I'm wicked tired with all the transferring and I need my body to come along too. Will ye help me or no?"

Emma didn't answer, she just pulled on her trousers and said, "Turn around."

"What?" said Callum confused.

"I need to change my top."

Callum realised that Emma was wearing one of his sister's nightgowns and she would have to take it over her head to put her own clothes back on. He turned around and started to empty some of his sister's clothes, and pack them under the bedclothes, making a sort of body shape.

"What are you doing?" asked Emma.

"My ma is a nurse, she'll look in on you every two or three hours you know. I'm hoping that this'll fool her."

Without speaking Callum took Emma by the hand, into his own bedroom and then down the pipe to the garden for the third time that night. Callum was quietly impressed with Emma. He wasn't sure that if he had gone through what Emma had tonight, that he would be able to shimmy down a drainpipe so well. Callum opened the shed door and picked up the fuel can for the boat and the spare oil and the backpack that he always kept packed that would help if there were an emergency on the boat. They ran down to the quayside, meeting no one. If anyone had been looking they would have seen two young adolescents holding hands running under the five orange streetlights looking for all the world like they were off to have fun and make mischief. Whoever had been watching would have had no idea of the fear in their hearts, and the trepidation in their minds.

The boat started with no problem (he remembered to open the breathe hole) and Callum motored out of the bay along Bull Hole. He knew this part of the coast so well he really did think he could navigate it in complete darkness, but tonight they were blessed with scudding clouds and a weak sliver of moon. While they were racing along Callum brought Emma up to date with his evening's work, and she started to cry again.

"I'm sorry," she said. "I know it's not your fault. I think they tracked us down through my searches on the internet. They would have thought it was my dad. I wasn't careful enough and I put them in danger and blamed you. It's not your fault. Thank you for doing this Callum."

"Aye, well you didn't know there was any danger until you learned of the French girl, so you shouldn't blame yourself."

"Thank you. I know you are right."

While they talked, Callum showed Emma how to drive the boat, how to replenish the fuel from the petrol can, adding oil in a 20:1 mixture. He showed her how to use the radio and the flares in the emergency bag and he told her about turning the boat to face the waves if they got big. He showed her the hand pump on the side of the boat and how the lifejackets that they were both wearing worked. All the while he was speeding towards the Island of Staffa. Seven miles from Fionnphort the island was clearly the direction the other boat had been going in before he had had to turn the owl back to land, and now he had passed that point. What if the other boat had changed direction? They must be at least an hour and a half behind and the trail would be fading if it was still there at all. Now they were out at sea the waves were beginning to crest and Callum was scared that he wouldn't be able to find the other boat. At last he saw what he was looking for. A guillemot was scared by the boat and started to take flight. Although a daytime bird they often overnighted on the waves and Callum presumed they could see reasonably well if they were prepared to fly at night.

"Follow that bird," was all Callum had time to say as he thrust the tiller into Emma's hands and focussed.

Well this thing was no owl when it came to night vision, but it seemed happy enough. They were about half way to Staffa now and Callum wheeled higher to see if he could spot the trail. Was that it? If it was it was still heading to Staffa, but the wind had picked up, as had the swells and Callum could no longer be certain. Still Staffa was the best bet. Why head towards Staffa if you didn't intend to go to Staffa? Callum knew there were countless reasons but he drove them from his head.

He looked down and could see Emma looking straight up at him, with wide, scared eyes. Suddenly, she looked like a twelve year old girl, in a small wooden boat, three miles from land looking for her parents, in the North Atlantic with a wind picking up, who were probably dead already. What on earth did he think they were doing?

He wheeled and flew down to sit next to Emma on his own body. The guillemot wasn't keen but soon settled down, with only the occasional internal scream of panic. Every so often he took off and checked their direction, and every time he did he was less certain than before that this was the right direction. About a quarter of a mile away from Staffa he flew down to Emma and pecked at the kill button, the button that turned the motor off and Emma understood that she was to wait there in a steadily rising chop. She reached out her hand and he pecked gently at it, before taking off, heading towards the dark forbidding cliffs of Staffa.

Staffa is about a mile all the way around and it only took Callum a few minutes to find what he was looking for. Around the north end of the island he saw a fishing boat that he didn't recognise anchored a few hundred yards offshore. This was not what you expected to see at this time of night, in this place. Far from where the tourists would be swarming tomorrow this place could be on the moon for all its nearness to Americans called Randy with their video cameras.

As he watched, an inflatable boat with a small outboard pulled out of what appeared to be a cave in the north west wall of the island. It was struggling a little in the waves that were now crashing against the rocks, but eventually it made its way out to the fishing boat. Two men got out of the inflatable and dragged it on board and then the fishing boat started its engines and to Callum's huge relief continued past the island and didn't go back towards Fionnphort. If it had, it would have been bound to have seen Emma sitting with what looked like a corpse in a small boat. Instead, it started to motor towards Ulva, the nearest safe harbour in a storm.

Callum was preparing to fly down to the cave when he felt the guillemot pressing in on him. Having done this three times that evening already, and each time to his advantage, he took the time to search for the guillemot and mix with its psyche. The guillemot was scared. Not immediately scared, but it wanted to…it wanted to fly to the other side of the island. Callum didn't know why, he could feel clearly the course of action that the bird wanted to take but he couldn't figure out the messages he was getting. They didn't make sense to a human mind. "Soon, my friend" he soothed the bird and swooped down to see inside the cave.

The cave was about 6 or 7 metres long and was made of the columnar basalt that makes Staffa famous. The caves, including the Great Fingal's Cave that all the tourists come to see, is made when faults, great cracks in the earth's surface are eroded by the sea. They form a weakness that is exploited by the relentless pounding of the waves over centuries wearing away at the rock until a cave is born. Unlike most caves, the bottoms are not sandy or rocky, but they are deep gashes where the only place to be is on the side walls where half columns give a foot and hand hold. It was halfway back inside the cave on the left-hand side perched on the top of a basalt column that Callum could see Professor and Mrs Higgins. The professor seemed hurt, with blood seeping from his head and dripping into the water. Mrs Higgins was looking around, looking for a way of escape, while holding on to her husband.

The genius struck Callum forcibly. If you wanted to kill someone, what a great way to do it! The tide was coming in. In a few minutes they would be washed from their perch and be smashed repeatedly against the walls of the cave until, bloody and mashed, a predator would come and start to nibble on the flesh. Eventually the bodies would be gone, and if by some freak of sea, a body should turn up on a beach somewhere, the post mortem would reveal only drowning as the cause of death.

Callum knew that if the Higgins were to be saved then he had to move fast. The waves were already washing at their feet. He flew out of the cave and back to Emma. The fishing boat was taking its time to clear the area but if he and Emma didn't hurry, the Higgins were finished.

Back in his own body Callum was shocked by two things. The first was how tired he was. The transferring was taking its toll and he could barely stir himself to start the engine and turn towards the cave. The second thing was the size of the waves. Emma was looking terrified and she was already manning the pump. At last he realised what the bird had been saying to him. A storm was coming and it wanted to ride it out in the lee of the island. So much for 'red sky at night'.

He explained the situation quickly and while Emma was hugely relieved to hear that her mother and father were still alive, she could tell by the look on Callum's face that it might not be for long. They covered the distance to the mouth of the cave in only five or six minutes and could still see the navigation lights of the fishing boat disappearing into the gloom.

Callum took one look at the cave and said, "Emma, I'm sorry. I'm really sorry. To go in there is suicide. Your parents wouldne want you to do that." Callum was sure that he would have to argue with Emma, but she could see the sense in what he was saying. The mouth of the cave was a maelstrom of boiling white foam and surging waves.

"To come so close... Is there nothing we can do?" asked Emma in a tragic whisper that was breaking Callum's heart.

If this was going to work, it would be the luckiest thing that had ever happened to Callum. If this worked he was going to go straight out and buy a lottery ticket. Why would a large bull seal be swimming around out here? Even if he could find one, or just sense one, he would have to go in twice and he didn't know if a bull seal could drag a person out of a cave and swim them to Iain's boat whilst holding them out of the water. Still, he had to try for Emma's sake.

Callum focussed. He could feel his mind go out from the boat through the water, across to the waves and the rocks, deeper into the sea. His mind was searching. He would know it when he found it. He came across many sentient creatures, mainly fish, but he couldn't find what he was looking for...there!

He felt the usual nausea for only a second now and even managed the thought that he was getting good at this.

Perhaps he wasn't as good as he thought as he realised that he had transferred into a young small seal. He guessed that meant that there couldn't have been a bull seal around. He was worried that he wouldn't have the strength in this smaller body to pull the mass that was Professor Higgins. It was all he had so he would do his best and try to work with it. He swam as fast as he could towards the cave. There was no fear now. The sea was his element and a few waves on the surface didn't bother him! He flew into the cave to see and feel his worst nightmare. The two Higginses who had been on a ledge were now in the water. They were in the very back of the cave around a small dogleg. It was giving them some protection, but every wave crashed them onto the rocks. Their death was only a matter of time, and very little of that. As Callum was considering the next move the seal's consciousness screamed into his own. Taken by surprise, he merged with the seal and let it do what it wanted, and what it wanted was to flee. As it shot out of the mouth of the cave Callum caught a glimpse of a huge smiling face. A huge smiling black and white face, and Callum was gripped with the same mind-numbing fear that was filling the young seal he had transferred into. He had only seen one of these behemoths in these waters once before although he knew they were regular Hebridean visitors. The orca or killer whale is the largest sea mammal found in these waters and its diet consisted of seal. Callum looked behind him to see the huge mammal open its jaws with a meal on its mind.

FOCUS!

Just in time Callum, now in the orca, closed his jaws on nothing and he felt the disappointment deep in the orca's mind. This was a young animal and it was hungry. Callum presumed it had been attracted by the smell of the Professor's blood in the water.

Callum turned the great beast back towards the cave. The orca didn't like the manoeuvre that Callum was attempting. He knew that orcas don't swim backwards, and it was going to be a tight fit in the cave, but he had to try!

Callum manoeuvred the orca so that it was facing out of the cave, slowly being washed back into the cave by the waves. If this worked, it would be a miracle.

Afterwards when they were talking to the police about what had happened, the Higgins decided that that was exactly what it was. It was a miracle. It was clearly difficult for them to accept, both of them being devout atheists, but what other explanation was there?

Mrs Higgins was battered and bleeding but was still in better shape than her husband. She only had a broken rib. His head was badly cut and he kept drifting in and out of consciousness. Mrs Higgins had also felt an ominous crack when a particularly large wave had smashed them against an underwater pillar, and she thought that her husband's leg was broken. She knew they were going to die. How could they not? Their situation was beyond desperate. It was hopeless. She didn't even know why they were being put to death in such a gruesome manner. Their captors had worn masks and hadn't spoken a word.

Mrs Higgins was preparing herself to let the professor sink and herself with him when she saw, backing down the cave towards her the two-metre dorsal fin of a killer whale. What made her do it she never worked out. Perhaps it was because it looked like a giant dolphin, (which is exactly what a killer whale is), and everyone has heard the tales of dolphins saving drowning sailors. Perhaps because it was the only thing she could hold on to.

Whatever the reason, she grabbed the tail of the beast and pulled herself and her husband up the back and onto the dorsal fin. The professor seemed to know that he had to hold on and he did. The great beast then started to swim out of the cave, slowly so as not to wash them off and towards what looked like a little boat.

Callum was close to passing out with exhaustion. When he felt the Higgins on his back he didn't feel like he had the strength to will the orca to swim back to the boat. He felt himself blacking out for moments and then coming to all whilst still in the mind of the orca, but he managed not to lose control of the beast, the beast that could so easily kill them all. Too many transfers were killing him.

When Mrs Higgins got to the boat she found her daughter, tiredly thrusting the handle of a pump backwards and forwards, losing the battle to keep the sea out of the boat. Next to her was the friend she had made, Callum. He looked worryingly ill or even dead. His face was white and sallow, and he didn't seem to be breathing at all. The whale she was sitting on lifted its great black back so that she and her husband could slide into the boat and then it slid, without a whisper, beneath the waves. There didn't seem to be anything to say. They were all too tired. Emma had come all this way in the middle of the night to rescue them, and as unlikely as it seemed, with the help of the whale, had done so. Out of all the craziness of the last few hours probably the thing that stuck in Mrs Higgins' mind the most was that Emma didn't seem scared at all by a vast marine mammal dumping her parents into a small skiff in the middle of the night, not only did Emma not seem scared but not even surprised. It must have been the shock.

"What can I do Angel?" she asked her daughter.

"Pump mum."

Without further talk, Emma pulled the starting handle and the engine sputtered to life. Pointing the boat away from the island, roughly the way they had come, they sped off into the inky blackness and out to sea. Emma knew she had no idea how to get home and the waves were regularly breaking into the boat now. Come back Callum, I need you.

Callum was beyond tired. He was beyond exhaustion. He had no idea how he was keeping going. He only knew that he had to get this hungry flesh-eating carnivorous whale away from the boat before he let it go. With this in mind, he turned the beast away from the little boat with Emma and her parents in and headed after the fishing boat. As soon as he had turned he could feel new noise. He didn't have to be a whale to know what it was. The screw from the fishing boat was way too close. It must have turned around to come back. Maybe it was checking to make sure it had done the job, maybe it had seen their boat. Either way Callum could sense the boat bearing down on Iain's boat. Much heavier, it would crush the skiff and kill everyone on board while barely leaving a scratch on its own hull.

Anger coursed through Callum giving him a final burst of energy. After all he had done, how dare they kill them all in a 'boating accident'. He, Callum, would not allow it!

The orca hit the fishing boat with its massive head at 30 miles an hour, just below the waterline. The crunching of wood and fibreglass echoed around the skull of the whale. It took less than a minute for the boat to go down leaving the two men on board swimming, their legs enticing bait for a hungry orca. Callum left the orca heading slowly towards the men. This would be the easiest meal it had ever had. Definitely worth the headache.

Chapter 6

Wednesday Night to Thursday Morning Callum and Emma

Emma was struggling. With the extra weight in the boat, the waves were coming over the side and the boat was settling lower and lower in the water. The moonlight that had guided them out had gone behind clouds and it was pretty dark. All she could really see were the cresting waves, close together and irregular as the boat crashed through their peaks at an angle. The wind had been picking up and Emma wasn't sure that even after Callum's herculean efforts they would survive.

Emma felt Callum's hand pull at her arm to come closer. He looked in a bad way. She leaned in to catch his words.

"Radio…coastguard…say STAFFA…hear anything, use flares." He seemed to have finished talking but then grabbed her arm again. "Head into waves, go slowly."

With that he sank back on the floor of the boat and lapsed into unconsciousness.

Emma turned into the waves as Callum had instructed and reduced her speed. Immediately the boat stopped shipping water. The bows rode easily up and over the waves, and although the ride was a bit bumpy, Emma felt that they had a chance. After a few minutes, Emma's mum stopped pumping and Emma realised that the skiff was empty of water and riding higher. Emma checked the petrol and the oil and having sorted out the immediate dangers decided to do as Callum asked and call the coastguard. She opened Callum's emergency bag and took out the radio. It was a hand-held VHF radio which only worked in a line of sight. Emma remembered Callum's warning about how the coast guard got hundreds of false calls every year and how she should only call in an emergency.

Emma only needed to ponder for a tiny moment. She was sitting in a small boat that she barely knew how to control, with her dazed mother, and two unconscious casualties. They had an unknown amount of fuel, two miles out at sea probably heading towards America three thousand five hundred miles away into a gathering storm at midnight. She felt that that was emergency enough… she was going to make the call.

She turned the radio on and turned it to channel 16 as Callum had showed her. It really helped being a child genius…people only had to show her and tell her something once.

"Mayday, Mayday, Mayday. This is Iain's boat, Iain's boat, Iain's boat. Our position is Staffa, four persons on board, two unconscious, request immediate assistance, over."

Callum had said that there would always be a delay and either the coastguard would reply directly or someone else who was listening would reply and pass the Mayday on. This was how many Maydays got to the coastguard. While she was waiting, Emma mused on the derivation of the word Mayday. It wasn't a reference to the UK spring bank holiday. It was an example of how words were adopted by other languages and changed over time. It started life as 'M'aidez', French for 'help me', and it has become the international call for help. All people and all languages now use 'Mayday' when they need to call for help.

"Iain's Boat, Iain's Boat, Iain's Boat, this is the coastguard. All other traffic clear this channel until further notice. Now then lassie, is that Emma?"

Emma breathed a sigh of relief. "Yes, this is Emma."

"Let me speak to Callum lass. Over."

"I can't, he's unconscious. Over."

"Let me speak to your father then. Over."

"I can't he's unconscious as well. Over."

"Your mother, then, over," the radio crackled in growing frustration.

Emma silently handed the radio over to her mother and mimed pressing the button to speak.

"This is Mrs Higgins."

"Aye, it's good to hear from you madam, what's the situation there? Over."

"There is no point asking me," said Mrs Higgins, "I know nothing about boats. Emma is in charge here." Without saying anything else or waiting for a reply, Mrs Higgins passed the radio back to Emma.

"We are facing into the wind, but I don't know what direction that is. I have reduced the speed and checked the fuel. There is no water in the boat and we are shipping only a little that the pump is coping with I think we'll be OK for a few minutes, but can you hurry, my dad is hurt, and I don't know about Callum. Over."

"Well, lassie, it sounds to me like ye've got it all under control. The lifeboat has launched while we've been talking, GPS has a fix on you, and it should be with you in 8 minutes. Hang on there lassie. I'll be here if you need me. Out."

The radio went dead, and the only sound was the slapping of the waves and the whine of the wind which could now be heard over the drone of the outboard. Emma looked at her mother, she looked tired and old, but not scared anymore. She put her hand on her mother's arm. "It'll be fine now mum."

It seemed an age that Emma and Mrs Higgins sat in the boat, both lost in their thoughts, calmer now that they knew that help was on the way. Emma was worried about how she might avoid the questions that were inevitably coming her way and Mrs McBride wondering who had taken them and why…and what had Emma got herself mixed up in this time?

Seven and a half minutes later they heard the noise of another engine. A big powerful engine, going flat out.

Emma remembered Callum's instructions and took a flare from the emergency bag. She read the instructions and turned the handle through 90 degrees and then hit the bottom of the tube hard with the flat of her hand. The flare ignited. It was a white star burst flare that shot from her hand 60 metres into the air where it burned brightly for a time before falling back to the sea. They could hear a change in the tone of the engine and seconds later the skiff was dwarfed by the seven metre Rigid Inflatable Boat (RIB) that was the inshore lifeboat stationed at Fionnphort and coxswained by; Emma's heart jumped into her mouth when she saw the mountain that was Mr McBride sitting in the centre of the jockey console in front of the steering wheel.

The operation was extremely slick and it seemed like no time at all before her father and Callum where laid out on stretchers, and her mother was wrapped in a shiny survival blanket. One of the crew stepped nimbly into the skiff and having checked the fuel situation, opened up the engine and headed in a direction that Emma presumed led back to Fionnphort.

A blanket was wrapped around her shoulders and Mr McBride's deep, gravelly and enormously reassuring voice said, "Did ye know that there are over three hundred things that can happen to ye in a small boat and tha over half of them can kill ye?"

"Yes, I did. Thank you for coming to get us Mr McBride."

"That's al reet lassie. Ye did a gud job there lassie. When the lad weks up I'm sure he'll be reet proud. Now sit yoursen doon here and hold on." Having exhausted his repertoire of conversation Mr McBride sat Emma on the centre console and opened up the twin 150 horsepower Yamaha engines and the RIB lifted and started to skim back to Fionnphort at an amazing speed hardly bothered by the waves which now looked small. One of the crew had examined both Callum and Professor Higgins and said enigmatically, "No need fer yon chopper Captain."

Mr McBride spoke into the head mic that was an integral part of his RNLI helmet and Emma could hear him tell the coastguard that they wouldn't need the RAF Sea King helicopter, the casualties could receive first aid at Fionnphort, and then anyone who needed it could go to the Accident and Emergency department at the hospital at Salen. There would be an ambulance waiting at Fionnphort when they got there.

A few minutes later the RNLI RIB pulled up to the quay in Fionnphort and unloaded its casualties. There was quite a reception committee with Angus, Seamus, Morag, Mrs Doherty (of course) and what seemed like the entire clientele of the Keel Row. Arc lights had been set up on the quay so the ambulance crew could see what they were doing. It looked like a travelling circus and all Emma wanted to do was run and hide.

After the first aid and gas and air was administered to Professor Higgins, the paramedic (with Mrs McBride definitely getting in the way) examined Callum. "There's not wrong wi''im that I can find Mrs McBride. Do ye want to tek him home?" Without a word Mr McBride picked Callum up like he weighed nothing at all and walked the 300 metres to the house.

There wasn't enough room in the ambulance for all three Higgins, and Mrs Higgins was obviously torn between going with her husband and staying with Emma.

"You'll be off wi yer man then dearie!" said Mrs McBride when she sensed Mrs Higgins' indecision. "The wee lassie will be fine wi me here. She'll no escape from ma hoose agin!"

So it was settled, and Emma walked back up to the cottage she had left only a few hours earlier. Mrs McBride ushered her straight upstairs while Mr McBride carried Callum straight up to his room. Emma was certain that she wouldn't sleep with the excitement of the night's events, and she wanted to sneak into Callum's room to say thank you. Everyone else thought that she was the hero and that Callum was a wuss who had flaked out. Only she knew how much Callum had done for her parents. She knew that she would never be able to repay such a huge debt, but she could try. She could use every tool at her disposal to find Callum's real mum. Emma fell asleep almost immediately, the last thing she heard was the raised voice of constable Green clearly on the phone to her mother, "…an orca ye say Mrs Higgins? An orca backed inte the cave and pulled ye both oot? Aye well, perhaps it has been a very long night and mebbe I should be tekkin this statement in the mornin'."

Emma smiled, lay her head back on the pillow and slept for twelve straight hours.

Callum had never felt so tired in his life before. It wasn't as if he had been exercising too much or even as if he had been thinking for too long. It was a feeling as if something

118

had entered his body and drained the energy from every cell. He had a vague memory of leaving the Orca and regaining his body. He knew he had spoken to Emma about what to do next. He presumed she had carried out his instructions because his next memory was of being carried up the stairs to his room by Mr McBride. His mum came into his room and shooed everyone else out.

"Mum. Is everyone OK?"

"Aye lad, wi time all will be well. Now go te sleep."

"Did Iain's boat mek it OK?"

"Aye lad, Now go te sleep."

"Have the police found the two kidnappers?"

"Enough Callum. GO TO SLEEP!"

Callum looked up at Mrs McBride who ruffled his blond hair and smiled. "Ye and yon lassie did a gud thing tonight Callum. Now sleep! Oh and Callum? How did ye ken that there were two kidnappers?"

Mrs McBride never did get an answer as Callum was fast asleep.

Callum woke at 11 o'clock the following morning, with the sun streaming in through his window. He had slept well for part of what was left of the night, but as others started to rise and move around the house, his sleep became troubled with disturbing dreams. Dreams of him smashing his own head into the fishing boat while the two kidnappers laughed and pointed behind him at a two-metre dorsal fin, racing towards him. Callum woke with the realisation that he had killed two people. They were bad people who had tried to kill Emma's mum and dad, but did that give him the right to kill them? Callum realised that he could kill, by transferring to an animal, anyone at any time and no one would know it was him. If the animal was found it would be destroyed but he would never get caught. The more he thought about it, the more he realised that being a teletransferer in a world where nobody believed it was possible meant that he was a very powerful individual, and with that power came temptation. He could steal at will, he could get to places no one else could, he could commit the perfect crimes.

Callum came to full wakefulness when his door was opened quietly by..."Iain! What are ye doin here?"

"Shhh, lad. I don't want the others to know that we've spoken!"

"When did ye get back? I thought that ye weren't comin' 'til the end o' the week?"

"Aye lad," Ian replied quietly. A long few seconds passed while Iain looked wonderingly at Callum. He looked like he was coming to a decision in his mind and needed a few seconds to be certain.

"Who knows about ye, and what ye can do?" asked Iain quietly.

"What do ye mean?" asked Callum while a cold chill ran down his spine under the bedclothes.

"I know what ye can do." Was Iain's knowing reply. "I know aboot the animals an all."

"What do you mean, the animals?" Callum asked innocently, stalling for time. Just for a moment doubt crossed Ian's forehead, putting two furrows between his striking black eyebrows. Obviously taking after his father, Iain equalled Mr McBride's height but was clean shaven and had a smaller, more athletic frame. He was dressed incongruously in a grey suit with a red checked tie which Callum had only just noticed. Iain must be working, concluded Callum.

The doubt in Iain's face was gone as quickly as it arrived and this time he spoke with more conviction.

"Callum. I know that you can 'be' in other animals. I know that ye were in that orca last night and the dolphin the other day. I also know that other people will work out that it's you and then they will try to kill you. I havne worked out why the Professor and his wife were teken, but I suspect that it has something to do with you and your friendship wi' Emma. Callum, ye don't have te say oot, but I know. I need ye to trust me to help protect ye. I need te know who else knows."

Callum wasn't sure quite what was happening. How on earth could Iain know? Callum had hardly seen him for the last few years and now he claims to know something that Callum himself had only learned a few days previously.

Callum knew he needed to tell someone else, and although they had had their differences, Iain had been older by enough such that they had remained friends, so Callum told Iain everything. The buzzard, the rabbit, meeting Emma, the internet and the boat chase the previous night. It took twenty-five minutes and by the end of it Iain looked incredulous.

"So it is true. It's so easy not to believe…" Iain said half aloud. "This is incredible…" Iain stood up quickly and turned to Callum. "Callum, ye have to listen to me. I need to tell you a secret as well. I'm not just a CID officer, I'm summat else as well. I was recruited as I joined the police into another organisation, a secret organisation. I have been trained well but I have only one assignment reet now. You, Callum. My job is you. Mainly to protect you, and I'm sorry that last night I nearly failed ye. If I am to do my job ye must promise not to tell anyone else at all aboot what ye can do. Ye must tell no one and ye must stop doin it. It will get ye noticed and it will get ye killed. Tell no one." Iain turned to go but was stopped by Callum's "Wait! What secret organisation?"

"Ask yer new friend Callum, she's well known to us," and with that he turned and left.

Callum got up and wandered downstairs. Everything seemed so normal. Callum wasn't sure what he had expected, but it wasn't this. PC Green had left to 'continue his enquiries', apparently muttering that the bigwigs from Glasgow had turned up making, his job harder. Mr McBride was piloting the ferry, and Mrs McBride was waiting for him in the kitchen with what smelled like a mighty breakfast. Over that breakfast, Callum learned from Mrs McBride that four policemen, including Iain, had flown in first thing this morning by helicopter, which was still parked at the Columba Centre. Apparently, they had commandeered the island's police vehicles and were driving around taking statements and generally getting in everybody's way. In other news (there was plenty of it), the lifeboat was out with Seamus as cox, looking for a fishing boat based in Oban that had disappeared the previous night. It had two fishermen on board, both of whom had wives and children. As he heard this Callum felt sick. He felt guilt such as he had never felt before. They were dead, both of them, because of him. What right did he have to take their lives? He calmed himself with the thought that nature seemed to have a 'kill or be killed' philosophy and they had tried to kill his friend's family.

After that, he hung around the house waiting for Emma to wake up. When she did, he had to wait while Mrs McBride told her she couldn't go back to her house and that she would be staying with them for a few days until the police had finished their investigation and the house had been cleared up a bit.

"The police will want to talk to both of ye as well. You'd best get yer stories straight. Yer mother had a wild tale of an orca swimming in to the cave and draggin them oot. Yer brother, Cal, he thought that she must've had a wee bang to the heed. Now go oot from unda ma feet. It's a bonnie day agin."

Callum and Emma walked to the top of Catchean where they had first met only a few days before. They sat looking at Iona, laid out before them. It was a beautiful summer's day, nearly 20°C, the sun was shining, and even though the temperature wasn't that high, they could feel the power of the sun through their shirts. The growing season is quite short on Mull. In the winter it can be dark for up to 17 hours a day, so the local flora and fauna almost hibernate, so when the summer comes and the sun can rise at 4.30 am and set at 11 pm everything bursts into life and Emma and Callum were surrounded by insects busily collecting the nectar that would sustain them through the long cold winter. Flowers were in bloom everywhere including the rare and beautiful orchids only found in that part of Scotland.

Emma tentatively took Callum's hand and held it tightly in her own.

"Thank you, Callum."

"Aye, well…you're welcome I guess. I don't know what to think about those fishermen. I think they're lost. I think the orca got them."

Emma looked a bit aghast at Callum who couldn't meet her eyes.

"Were you still in the orca when it, when you, when it …killed them?" she asked in a quiet voice.

"No, I was in the orca when it smashed their boat though. It was me that put them in the water. They were going to run you down. They were going to kill all of us! There was nothing else I could do! Nothing!"

"It's alright Callum. You did the right thing. They forfeited their rights when they tried to kill my parents. It was self-defence. You did the right thing. Besides, if you weren't in the orca when it, when it killed them, then it wasn't you was it? It was the orca!"

"The orca wouldn't have had a chance if I hadne smashed their boat," said Callum morosely.

"Maybe the storm would have got them. By the time the RIB got back the waves were pretty big, and the wind was blowing very hard."

"No, the storm last night was only a baby. They would have been out in a lot worse."

The two twelve year olds sat on top of the hill looking out over the bay, both lost in their own thoughts, but clutching each others' hands tightly, bound by a secret, and a shared trauma.

After half an hour or so, during which they gazed at the incredible 360 degree view, they could hear a wheezing and muttering coming up the hill from the village and, just as they were getting scared that perhaps some vast lumbering bear had escaped from a zoo and made its way to Fionnphort, they saw Mr McBride come over the brow of the hill with his head down and his hands pushing on his knees, struggling to the top. Callum couldn't remember Mr McBride ever walking up the hill before. Emma snatched her hand back before Mr McBride could see it in Callum's hand, much to the relief of Callum.

"Are ye alreet pa?"

"Aye, I'm alreet. Why wouldna be?" wheezed Mr McBride, lowering himself on to a nearby rock and looking like a prime candidate for a heart attack.

"Callum, one of yon polissmen needs to tek a statement from the pair of ye. Apparently Iain canne do it because he's yer brother."

"Come on then Emma, we'd better go down" said Callum standing to go. Emma stood as well, and they turned round expectantly to the still wheezing Mr McBride. "Yous go on doon, I'll stay here awhile and look at yon view."

Emma and Callum started down the hill only to be stopped by Mr McBride shouting. "Oh, and Callum lad! Ye'll be pleased ta know that they found the two of them. The ones that took the Professor and his wife. They were in a life raft drifting off Lunga. It was a wee bit odd. When the helicopter picked them up they were talking aboot an orca as well. They're safely locked up in Oban! I'll see you doon at the hoose in a wee few minutes!"

It was with a song in his heart that Callum practically skipped back down the hill towards the house. The orca hadn't eaten them! They were still alive, and their wives had husbands and their children had fathers. Now they can rot in gaol for the rest of their lives!

"What are we going to tell the police?" asked Emma.

"We canne tell them about me, because it could be dangerous and because they won't believe us anyway," said Callum. "Would you be able to lie for me Emma? I know you said that you always tell the truth, but I heard you lie to your dad when I left your house the night before last when your parents came home. So can you lie again?"

"I didn't lie at all!" exclaimed Emma. "If you think carefully about what I said, it was the truth. I had felt ill earlier and although I thought you would come round, I couldn't have known you would! I told you I don't lie, I find it very difficult to do."

"Oh," said Callum, who was very tempted to tell Emma about his conversation with Iain earlier.

"What I am very good at," said Emma with a twinkle in her eye, "is not telling the whole truth. Don't worry Callum, I'll find a way to keep your secret."

The police were waiting for them in the sitting room and it felt like a very grave situation indeed. The curtains were drawn, and Mrs McBride was sitting bolt upright in her chair with a very serious look on her face.

"Emma, yer mum has agreed that I can step in as a 'responsible' adult while yer interviewed by the poliss. This is Detective Sergeant Karen Reeve. All ye have to do is tell the truth and all will be well. Sergeant."

"Thank you Mrs McBride. Come and sit down you two. We will be taking separate statements, but you can give them together if it helps us get the truth."

Sergeant Reeve was a pretty brunette, in her mid-thirties who looked good in the uniform, Callum couldn't help noticing her smile. She was obviously English, and Callum wondered why an English policewoman would want to be stationed in Glasgow.

"Callum. I'd like you to start by telling me exactly why you and Emma went out in your brother's boat when you had been told not to."

Callum thought her smile wasn't so pretty now.

"I knew that Emma was worried aboot her folks and I thought that mebbe we could have a wee look along the coast to see if we could see them. Angus… I mean Constable Green, was here and nobody was oot looking for them."

Sergeant Reeve wrote in her notebook and didn't seemed particularly pleased.

"Why didn't you ask your parents if you could go?"

Callum thought that that was, not only a daft question but also a bit mean.

"Because they would have said no," answered Callum sheepishly.

Sergeant Reeve turned to Emma and said, "I understand from your mother that you always tell the truth?"

"I never tell lies," said Emma with complete conviction.

"Why did you and Callum go out in the boat?"

127

"I went in the boat with Callum because he wanted to look for my parents."

"Why did you go towards Staffa?"

"Callum said that he had seen evidence of a fishing boat going that direction. He said it was unusual, so we followed it."

"When you got to Staffa what did you do?"

"We drove the boat around the island and Callum saw an inflatable tender come out of a cave."

"What did you do then?"

Callum waited with his heart pounding. Emma had told the truth until now. She had been careful to leave bits out, but it had all sounded plausible. This was going to get tougher.

"I waited like Callum told me to. Callum then drove the boat to the mouth of the cave. After a while, my mum and dad got in the boat and Callum told me to head back to Fionnphort and call the Coastguard."

"Your mum told me that she and your dad were rescued by an orca. What do you think of that?"

"It isn't very likely is it?" asked Emma. "What did my dad say?"

"Your dad said that he didn't remember anything about it at all. His first memory is being transferred into the RNLI RIB. Did you see an orca?"

"Yes"

"What was it doing?"

"It was swimming around by the cave."

"Your mum says that it picked them up in the cave. Did you see that?"

Callum winced.

"No," said Emma.

"Why do you think your mum said that it did?"

"I think she told you exactly what she thought happened," said Emma emphatically.

"Your mum had had a traumatic time, do you think she could have imagined the orca saving her and your dad?"

Emma sat silently for a few seconds, obviously thinking hard.

"I think that my mum has a wonderful imagination. I don't have a good imagination, but my mum does. I think that she is perfectly capable of imagining something like that."

"Thank you Emma. Now Callum, the fishermen claim that the orca rammed and sank their boat. Did you see that?"

Callum had been impressed with Emma's ability to tell the truth and yet pass no useful information at all. While she was answering the questions they sounded to Callum like a complete pack of lies until he listened very carefully. When he did that, he realised that Emma was answering the literal question and not what was meant by the question. He would have to be very careful when asking Emma questions in future. He decided that it had worked very well for her and so he would do exactly the same thing.

"Yes."

"So you're saying that you saw the orca ram the fishing boat?"

"No… Yes…No"

"Did you see the orca ram the fishing boat?"

"It was very dark."

"Callum, a simple yes or no will do."

This is too difficult. Emma is cleverer than me thought Callum. I'm just going to lie.

"No I didn't. Orcas don't ram fishing boats. I did see the orca but it didn't go into the cave and it didn't ram anything!"

"Why do you think Mrs Higgins said that the orca saved her and her husband?"

"I think she must have had a wee bang on the heed. She swam oot of the cave with the Professor, and I helped them into the boat. I was very tired and I think I fell asleep after I told Emma what to do wi the boat."

"Thank you Callum, Emma. I think that'll do. It sounds as if Mrs Higgins is a better swimmer than she thinks, and the fishermen hit a rock. Far more likely than the orca story!"

Chapter 7

Thursday Afternoon Callum

Having gone through the rigours of giving a police statement Callum and Emma went outside. The sun was still shining and life was going on all around them. The shop was busy, tourists were walking around doing touristy things like taking a million pictures they would never look at or delete. It felt surreal that they were caught up in anything sinister on such a beautiful day.

"What would ye like to do for the rest of the day, then?" asked Callum.

"What I really want to do is go and see my dad and then I want to get online and see who has been tracking my IP address. I want to know who kidnapped my parents and tried to kill them."

"Oh!" said Callum. "I was more thinking about whether you would like to go for a walk, or go over

131

to Iona or take the boat out…but if ye'd rather solve a kidnapping…"

"I want to go home" said Emma. "I'm not scared anymore now I know my parents are safe."

"Well, if you're sure…" said Callum, secretly wanting to do the same, "…besides, I have something to tell you."

It took just a few minutes to get up to the Higgins' house where they were greeted with an amazing sight. People were wandering in and out of the house carrying carpets, and curtains, and broken furniture. Even Mrs McDougall was carrying bunches of local heather into the sitting room.

"What…? What's happening?" asked Emma, obviously surprised and slightly concerned. Callum found that he wasn't surprised at all and had almost been expecting it.

One of the disadvantages of living in a tiny village on the end of a long peninsula stuck out on the bottom of a large island with only 150 people living there, was that everyone knew your business and wanted to interfere with it constantly.

One of the advantages of living in a tiny village on the end of a long peninsula stuck out on the bottom of a large island with only 150 people living there, was that everyone knew your business and wanted to interfere with it constantly.

The police had finished with the house mid-morning and the village had moved in to make it nice for the return of the family. All traces of the violence were being removed and, although it would take a while for some of the materials to be delivered from the mainland, within a few days the house would be free of all reminders of the horror of the crime that had been committed there.

"Why are they all in my house?" asked Emma, obviously confused by the presence of people she didn't know.

"They heard about what happened and they came to help," answered Callum.

"Why would they want to do that?" asked Emma still, obviously confused.

"Because that's what ye do in a small village. We help each other oot. Your family has had a tough time, so the others are helping you oot."

Emma just stood there looking dazed.

"But they don't know us."

"It happens all the time," said Callum patiently, "there's an English guy who moved to the village last year to take up fishing. He's nae gud, so the other fishermen share their catch with him so that he has somat to land and he can mek a living. Yon Mrs McTavish lives three miles away and can't get into the village to get her shopping, so the locals all tek it in turn to deliver, in the winter old Mr…"

"OK, OK, I get it," said Emma. "It's just that where I come from people wouldn't do that unless you knew them well."

"Welcome to Fionnphort!" said Callum smiling, "now let's see what it's like."

Callum led the way to the door that had been miraculously repaired. OK, it needed painting, but it was secure and looked so much better than it had the previous evening. Inside was the same. The carpets and curtains were gone but it was clean and all the mess had been taken away.

The broken glass had gone and there was a lovely smell coming from the kitchen.

"Just in time lass!" said Morag from the shop. "We're just finishing off and then we'll be oot of yer way, though I'll stay while ye've got young Cal wi you."

As Morag spoke, Mrs McDougall put down the flowers she had been carrying and made a beeline for Emma. Morag deftly intervened and hustled Mrs McDougall to the door with a "Thank you very much for all yer help now Mrs McDougall, I know you'll be wanting to get off now a busy woman like yourself!" Callum offered Morag a grateful smile and noticed with horror that Emma looked like she was going to start crying AGAIN!

"What now?" he asked. "I know it's not the same as it was and ye've lost the TV an all but it's not so bad!"

"It's not that…it's just so kind!" said Emma.

There was a noise from upstairs and Emma's voice clouded over, "Who's upstairs?" she asked.

"Why, I canne say!" replied Morag. "There's been that many people in and oot of here this morning. Run up and see will ye Callum? I'll mek us all a nice cup of tea. Come and sit yoursen doon lass."

Callum left Morag fussing over Emma who had appeared to recover from her nearly-going-to-cry episode. Callum was beginning to think that Emma was up and down like a buoy in a chop. Maybe it was just her, and maybe it was all girls. When Isla was at home she was just horrible in a big sister sort of way, so she hadn't helped with Callum's education of the opposite sex.

It took Callum only a few seconds to fly up the stairs and burst into Emma's room. "Mr Dougherty! What are ye doin in here?"

"I could very well be asking you de same ting young Callum!" said Mr Dougherty. "I was checking that everything is OK up here in the young lass's room, and it seems that the villains missed this room completely. Well I'll be on my way then." And with that he walked purposefullly down the stairs and out of the door.

"Emma!" shouted Callum, "come up here!"

"What is it?" asked Emma as she burst through the door.

"Seamus Dougherty was in here and he was looking at your computer. Look it's on! You didn't leave it on and we know that the kidnappers missed this room, so how did it get on?"

Emma sat at the desk and started tapping away on the keyboard. Callum was amazed at just how fast she could type and look at the screen at the same time. When he used a PC, it was with his eyes strictly fixed on the keyboard. He had often wondered which numpty had put the CAPS LOCK key next to the 'A'. How many times had he looked up at the screen to see that he had spent the last five minutes inadvertently typing in upper case because he had accidentally hit the CAPS LOCK key while typing? Emma looked up with a curious look on her face.

"The computer was turned on at 8.30 am this morning. I think that it would have been a police computer expert because they knew what they were doing. They tried to trace my internet surfing history, but I always delete that whenever I get off the PC. I've written a small program that deletes all my internet activity."

"I thought you could buy those now. Why would you want to write your own?" asked Callum.

"Because they don't ever allow for the physical effect on the media of writing into new disc space. You can think of a disc drive as a pad of paper. When you delete stuff all you are doing is deleting the title of the page you have written on. When you delete stuff with one of the programs you mentioned that you can buy, all you are doing is rubbing out everything you have written. The trouble is, that a skilled operator with the right tools can get it back just like you could with indented paper by putting another piece of paper on top and rubbing it with a soft pencil. What my program does is scribble all over the blank pages. Whoever looked at this computer tried to access all sorts of stuff, but they were concentrating on my internet surfing history. Don't worry though, they didn't get much. What is interesting is that they hacked your e-mail account. Look!"

Callum was amazed to see his internet e-mail account come up on the screen. "How did you do that?" he asked aghast. "I didn't," said Emma. "This was accessed at 8.42am this morning, these are pages stored in a log file that they wouldn't have known was being created while they interrogated my machine. I put it on so that I would know if my dad was looking at my PC again. These are the mails they looked at…"

Callum had a gnawing feeling that this wasn't going to be a good thing. There was a reason he didn't want Emma to see his e-mail, he just couldn't remember why that would be.

Callum was still tired after his previous evening's adventures and his mind just wouldn't tell him what it was. Emma was flicking through the e-mails in his sent box. How sad was that! The last ten were all to Andrew. All he ever did was tell him what was going on in the village. The last one he'd sent just told Andrew that he had met a... "NO! DON'T READ THAT!"

But it was too late. There on the screen was his e-mail to Andrew.

Andrew,

Met a new girl in Fionnphort, minging. Lots to tell you about my weird dreams. See you soon.

Callum

PS. Iain has lent me his boat... Cool.

Callum knew that Emma had read it. He also knew that she would never understand that you lied to your mates about girls all the time. He knew she would be upset, and he was bracing himself for the explosion when Morag shouted up the stairs.

"Cal, time to go lad. I havte get back to the shop and I canne leave ye here. Come on now, Oot!"

He had forgotten all about Morag.

"Emma, I..."

"Don't please Callum. I don't want to hear any more lies. Please go," said Emma in a quiet but firm voice.

"But I didn't mean it. I didn't want to tell Andrew that I liked you. I don't think you're a... you're a ming...minger." Callum pleaded.

"Cal! Don't mek me get yer ma!" came Morag's insistent shout from downstairs.

"Emma! Please. You don't understand!"

"You are right Callum. I don't understand why anyone would lie to one friend about another. I don't understand why you would say anything so horrible about me. You either lied to Andrew or you are lying to me. I am sorry but I can't deal with this. Please leave!"

"Emma!" Callum pleaded.

"Leave!" Emma's voice was quivering and she was pleading just as much as Callum had been a few seconds before.

"Ye heard her!" said Morag whose head had come around the door just in time to hear Emma's heartfelt plea. "Leave the lass alone. Her parents will be back home in aboot twenty minutes so ye needn't stay!"

Callum turned to go, kicking himself for sending the e-mail. Why did he have to lie so much? Everybody lied all the time! Teachers did it when they said his work was 'very encouraging'. His dad lied every time he went out with Mrs McBride when he said she was beautiful. She wasn't beautiful, she looked like Gimli off Lord of the Rings! His mother lied when she told terminal patients that everything would be OK. How many times had he heard people ask each other if they are OK and then hear the reply 'Aye, everything's fine' when sometimes it clearly wasn't. How many kids lied about what they had been doing when they got home from their friend's houses. Without the little lies, life would be so difficult to live! The little lies were like oil smoothing our way, giving us privacy and enabling us to live with the image we had painted of ourselves. Perhaps Emma couldn't do that? Perhaps Emma saw herself as she truly was? Callum remembered one of Mrs McBride's favourite sayings, "May God give us the grace to see ourselves as others see us". Perhaps Emma did see herself as others saw her, with all the human imperfections and character flaws. That would be a tough burden to carry.

Callum walked from Emma's house with his head down and his hands in his pockets. Before he knew it he was on top of his favourite hill where he had first met Emma, for the second time that day.

Probably for the first time in four days, (was it still only Thursday?), Callum felt he had the time to reflect on everything that had happened. His head was filled with all sorts of questions. Who had been behind the kidnapping and attempted murder of the Higgins? Was it the government who didn't want proof that teletransferring was real? If so, how did Iain fit in? Iain works for the government so did he orchestrate the attempt? He had said that he only had one assignment, which was him! If that was true, where was he now? How did he know about what Callum could do? What could he do to apologise to Emma? Why had searching for teletransferring on the internet got such a violent response? Lots of crackpot people had to be searching stuff like that all the time. Why was this so terrible? Why did HE have this ability? If it was genetic then someone else in his biological family could also do it couldn't they? How had this happened? If it wasn't the government, who was it? What could he do to get back on good terms with Emma?

Callum sat and passed the questions round and round his head. He was most disturbed by the possibility that his brother was somehow mixed up with the attempt on the lives of Professor and Mrs Higgins. As he sat there he found he was drawn to a single question more than any other. How? How was it that he could do what he could do? How did it work? Callum found that he really, really wanted an answer but the only person he trusted was angry and upset with him. He needed to make up with Emma. He needed to go and find her.

CHAPTER 8

LATE THURSDAY AFTERNOON
EMMA AND CARL

As soon as Callum had left, Emma knew she had got it wrong. She really didn't know why people lied all the time, but she knew they did. Why did she imagine that Callum would be any different? She wanted him to be different, but was it fair to expect him to be? Emma supposed that asking Callum not to lie would be like asking her to lie. Perhaps he didn't mean it after all then, they had only just met and she knew that she wasn't pretty like the other girls at school. She knew she wasn't ugly, but she never wore makeup and kept her hair short which made her look boyish. She knew all of that. Sometimes she had caught boys at school looking at her in a funny way. Her mum had said that it was because she was pretty, but Emma knew that mums lied to their kids all the time about how pretty or clever they were! IT WAS SO CONFUSING! Callum seemed to like her or why did he spend so much time with her? If he liked her, why did he tell his friend Andrew that she was a 'minger'?

Whenever Emma got confused she needed time to sort things out in her head, and that meant being alone. Her mum and dad had finally got used to it, but Callum wouldn't understand. He would think that she didn't want to see him again. Emma did want to see him again. He was the best thing that had happened to her in a long time. He felt like a...like a friend. Perhaps she finally had a friend. Perhaps she had had a friend.

Just as she was thinking that she should go and find Callum her parents got back and there was a lot of hugging with her mum (hugging with her mum wasn't too bad, but once her dad had tried to hug her and her mum had burst out laughing saying that we both looked so uncomfortable that maybe we should agree that we loved each other but just not in a 'huggy' way, and from then on Emma and her dad were excused from hugging which suited everyone just nicely), her dad just stood there like a lump of clay like he always did, shuffling from foot to foot, (tricky in the cast he had from his ankle to his groin), and he did look a bit silly with tweeds and a head bandage.

"Angel" pronounced her dad pompously, "I never got a chance to thank you for saving our lives," and with that he disappeared into his office to try and recover his work from the mess the kidnappers had made.

"Oh Angel!" sighed her mum as she sat on the sofa. "What have you got yourself into now?"

"What do you mean Mum?"

"The kidnappers weren't after us! They spent a long time looking at your dad's computer while we were tied up in here. Your dad thinks they may have been hired by some rival American university to steal his research! Can you imagine someone hiring hit men to steal your dad's latest research into 'The significance of 3rd century standing stones on 8th century religious paintings' or 'Hallucinogens in the South American indigenous population religious rites'? It never occurs to him that you have the same IP address. Angel, what have you been doing?"

This was a worry. Emma sometimes forgot that her mum was pretty clever. Sure, her dad was the Professor, but her mum was the clever one. Emma also knew that if the questioning went on for long she would tell her mum everything. She knew that her mum understood how to ask questions that would make it very difficult for her to avoid answering them. She could do nothing to fight her mum. A few more minutes and Callum's secret would be out, and Emma didn't know what her mum would make of the idea that her new friend could inhabit animals.

"What do you mean Mum?"

"Sorry Angel. Have you hacked into anyone else's computer?"

"Yes."

"Whose?"

"The Inland Revenue"

"Has anyone seen my papers?" demanded Professor Higgins as he strode into the room. "They were here when

143

we were taken. Those damnable villagers have thrown them away! Interfering busybodies! Damn them all! That's ten years research gone! I could lose my chair over this!" Professor Higgins carried on garbling what sounded like nonsense for a few more seconds. Mrs Higgins got to her feet sighing and led the Professor back into his study and Emma could hear her mother placating him. Even Emma could see that her mum (as she had often claimed) had two children to look after, not just Emma. It was obvious that her mother had found the missing papers but was going to be a while with her father, so Emma took the opportunity to flee back upstairs to her computer.

Emma reckoned that she had about half an hour to get as much information as possible before her mum got the truth out of her, and then probably confiscate her computer. Who knew what her mum would say about the whole teletransference thing? Emma just didn't know if her mum and dad would keep Callum's secret. Her dad would want to write a scientific paper on Callum and probably want to cut his head up to see how it worked. She had to find out who had tried to kill her parents and why, before then.

It took her 40 minutes. 40 minutes to track down what she was after. As soon as Emma got to her computer her fingers started flying over the keyboard. She decided that the weakest link would be in the thugs who actually perpetrated the crime. Somehow, they had to be paid. Payments would lead straight back to the paymaster. That would inevitably lead to the brains behind the operation, and she already had an inkling as to who that may be! Like all the best crime novelists say, 'follow the money!'.

Finding the names and addresses of the two kidnappers was the easiest thing. She got the names from the website of the local paper; Ben McPhee (39) and Daniel Stuttard (33). It was child's play to get back into the police computer and find their names and addresses, (they both lived in Oban on the mainland). From there she had to find their bank accounts. That was much harder. She spent ten fruitless minutes trying to hack into the local banks but decided she didn't have the time. Back into the National Crimes Computer and from there, into the criminal records of the two in question. They had been arrested five years ago in relation to an LSD smuggling operation but were never charged, and two years before that they were interviewed over the disappearance of a Lyndsay Smith from London, but again were never charged. Off and on over the years they had been under surveillance by the police but had never been caught at anything. Here it is! Known associates, wow, what a long list! YES! She was right! Doctor Christian Slack, the elusive Doctor Slack name crops up again!

LSD, Doctor Slack, disappearances, kidnapping, attempted murder and Callum. How did it all fit together?

Emma cast her eyes back to the screen and they opened wider. That was interesting. There was a hold on further investigation into Doctor Christian Slack put on the computer four years earlier. Emma checked the file that was associated with the hold and traced it back electronically but hit a firewall. Emma knew that she only had limited time so she didn't try to crack the firewall. What she was able to do though, was to see the origination of the firewall. The electronic signature was hardly hidden. In fact it was right in

145

your face. It was a warning to stop going any further. The signature was that of the Ministry of Defence in London.

The Ministry of Defence was the Government department that was being sued by the soldiers who had claimed to be able to teletransfer when they were experimented on in the 1990s. Callum was living proof that teletransference was real and if Callum were to turn up in court in a…well in anything that wasn't human, that would be bound to cost the Government millions in compensation! Millions in compensation was motive. Would a government kill to cover its tracks? Emma wasn't sure, but she certainly wasn't convinced that they wouldn't.

Was Doctor Christian Slack in the employ of the Ministry of Defence? Was HE prepared to kill to keep their dirty secrets?

Proof. If Emma could find proof, then she could contact MI6 and maybe they would protect her and Callum, and her family. If the TV was to be believed there is no love lost between the different government departments like the MoD, the Police, MI5 and MI6. She needed to find the evidence for the connection between McPhee and Stuttard and Doctor Slack. If she could do that and then find evidence for the connection between him and the Ministry of Defence, then she had proof! Money would be the link. Slack getting paid by the Ministry of Defence and McPhee and Stuttard being paid by Slack. She would have to hack the banks after all and that would take time.

"Emma, come downstairs please Angel I haven't finished talking to you!" called Mrs Higgins up the short flight of stairs.

Emma locked her machine and started slowly downstairs dreading the inquisition that was certain to follow. Just as she put her left foot onto the bare concrete floor of the lounge there was a bark and a scrabbling at the door.

Emma ran to the door and found the dog that Callum had transferred into the previous night sitting on her doorstep. What was its name? Lottie! That was it.

"It's OK mum, I know who she belongs to, I'll take her back!" and without giving her mum a chance to reply or protest she grabbed her coat and ran out of the door slamming it behind her.

"It is you isn't it Callum?" she panted as they ran down towards the quay.

"Woof"

"Not good enough," said Emma. "I need three woofs and a growl to make sure I'm not just chasing a silly dog!"

"Woof woof woof grrrr," obliged Lottie.

They ran full pelt down through the village towards the slipway for the ferry to Iona. A 12 year old girl and a labradoodle, they ran past the shop on the left and past the coaches for the tourists on the right. They skidded to a halt at the top of the old granite slipway where Iain kept his boat and it was obvious what Callum wanted her to do. Emma wasn't keen getting back into the boat where she had been so scared only the previous night, but it was a beautiful calm sunny day and Callum would be with her so… Emma ran down the slip after Lottie who sniffed at a lifejacket that Emma tried to put on. Drat! It wasn't the same as the lifejacket she had worn on the previous two occasions she had been out on the boat with Callum and

147

it was a bit trickier, she had to pass the strap through her legs before clipping all the ties together…it looked like the expensive ones you got on all the yachts. She undid the ropes and pulled the boat into the quay. Sure enough, there was Callum looking for all the world as if he was dead in the bottom of the boat. If anything, he looked paler than usual and he looked a bit silly wearing some posh deck shoes that she hadn't seen before.

"OK Callum, you can come back now! Let Lottie go home, she'll get into trouble as it is!"

Lottie shot off up the quay yelping with her tail between her legs, but Callum didn't come back as he had before. Instead, Emma heard splashing and looked round to see Sammy the seal, who was always hanging around the main slipway hoping for scraps off the tourists, splashing just in front of the boat. Emma was a bit annoyed now. She could understand why Callum didn't want to come to the house but there was no reason why he didn't come back now.

"Ha Ha Callum," she muttered as she followed Callum out of the harbour.

CHAPTER 9

THURSDAY MORNING CARL

The Doctor had been very annoyed with the bungling of the Higgins' kidnapping. Now it was going to be much more difficult than previously to get to the girl that was obviously the brains of the two. Carl had created a shadow of the girl's IP address by getting Doctor Slack's police contact to install a hidden program on the girl's PC earlier that morning and was able to watch any internet activity in real time, but the girl hadn't been online since the previous evening. The Doctor had told Carl that she had been staying with his long-lost twin, Callum. The police had been into the house and had tried to find out where the girl had been surfing, but they were really amateurs. All they had found was the simple stuff that he had been expecting. The girl, Emma, had covered her tracks well. Still it was handy that the Doctor had such good sources in the MoD and in the police. When she did go back online he would be able to see exactly what the girl, Emma, had been looking at. How much had the girl worked out he wondered. How clever was she? Had she managed to make the link between the testing on soldiers in the 90s and Callum's abilities? The copy of the police statements from Mrs Higgins and McPhee and Stuttard clearly added up to Callum being in the orca. It was a nice rescue thought Carl as he tried to imagine backing an orca into a cave in bad weather. Orcas and other intelligent mammals could be difficult to control when they were scared. Callum had shown some skill there, and so soon after discovering his talent. Perhaps it wouldn't be as easy as he thought to kill his brother. Carl knew that the thought of killing his brother should fill him with guilt and was curious to note that although he felt no guilt he was beginning to have some curiosity about him. Why had Callum not shown any teletransferring abilities until now? Anyway, it didn't matter. Carl didn't know Callum and so Callum was just another person that Carl didn't know. Millions of people died every day all around the world so why should Carl care about just one more?

Carl himself had been teletransfering since he was 6 and then only under strictly controlled conditions. After so many years practicing his skills he was as adept as any in controlling another creature. During the LSD trials, the soldiers had been given super high doses of LSD and under its influence, they had been able to teletransfer. Carl had been schooled well in his abilities and he knew that LSD is a semi-synthetic drug derived from lysergic acid and is found in ergot, a fungus that grows on rye and other grains. In its pure form, it is a white, odourless crystalline powder that is soluble in water, and it was this pure form that was given to the soldiers in an attempt to enhance their natural abilities. LSD (Lysergic Acid Diethylamide), Carl knew is a powerful hallucinogen. It's a drug which alters a person's perception of sights, sounds, touch etc., to the extent where hallucinations can occur, where the user sees or hears things that don't really exist. What the Ministry of Defence had found was that some of the soldiers were able to control the hallucinogenic effects and they were left with greatly enhanced senses of smell, touch, eyesight and hearing. It was felt that such enhancements would give them an advantage in covert operations. Unfortunately, the side effects of the drugs meant that some of the hallucinations were so realistic that some of the soldiers involved in the tests claimed that they were able to 'be' inside the heads of other animals. At the time the MoD were uninterested in these claims, even though reports of teletransference had also come from anthropologists in South America where the leaders of tribes would also take strong related hallucinogenic drugs which could make them enter a death-like trance. When they awoke, they reported 'flying with eagles' and 'running with monkeys'. The MoD ended the tests but turned a blind eye to the private activities of the pharmacologist who had previously run the trials on the soldiers, Doctor Christian Slack. When the lawsuit was filed by some of the surviving soldiers (there had been a few accidents while they got the doses right), the MoD found that they had to protect their 'unofficial' researcher on a number of occasions from investigations by the police and the Inland Revenue.

Carl smiled to himself. How ironic it was that they should be protected by their soon to be victim? When his task was over, the MoD would no longer want to protect them but would be powerless to stop them. Then the Doctor's work could be revealed, and he, Carl, would become the most famous person in the world. The only person in the world who could, at will, occupy the minds of other creatures. Callum could not be allowed to stand in the way of all he had worked for. He should have died at birth. The Doctor had made a mistake with that one. A mistake that he would have to rectify.

"Carl?" The Doctor had disturbed his musings. "What is your analysis of the situation that we find ourselves in?"

"Well Doctor, the boy Callum poses no immediate threat to our plans except that if he talks and proves his abilities, we will undoubtedly lose the support of the MoD. They will be worried about the damages claim. I am more concerned about the girl. She appears to be of above average intelligence, and although I am unable to determine exactly what she knows, I fear that the arrest of our two associates from Oban may give her a trail to follow that could conceivably lead to you. If she were able to do this then there could be unfortunate consequences leading to a delay in our final goal."

"And what is your solution to this unfortunate turn of events?"

"Doctor, I am afraid that we will have to terminate both the boy Callum and the girl, Emma, but before we do that we must stop her finding out any more and communicating it to anyone. To do that, we must stop her internet access. I have tried from here but the security at British Telecom has improved to the extent that I am unable to kill it electronically. Would it be possible for one of your thugs to do it the old-fashioned way? If you can organise that, I will arrange for Miss Higgins to be brought here and if I arrange it carefully enough, Callum will follow. We can then deal with them ourselves."

"Carl, as I believe I have said more than once, your ability to analyse a situation and prioritise the appropriate actions has become of much use to me. I am genuinely fond of you and your ruthlessness. Unfortunately, I cannot agree entirely with you on this occasion. Terminating the boy would be an error. Firstly, he is being watched by his adopted brother, who as you know works for MI6 and who has undoubtedly filed a report already, and secondly, he is the only other teletransferer that we know of, and therefore he is the perfect stand-in for you if anything should happen. I feel that killing the boy would bring too much trouble our way at this stage of the operation. Terminate the girl but keep the boy alive."

"As you wish Doctor."

"How will you bring the girl to us?"

"Trust, Doctor. People trust and that is their weakness. To be dependent on another is a failing that the truly great figures from history did not have. Emma trusts Callum."

As Carl stood up to leave, the Doctor smiled. Carl would get Emma and Callum here. He would find out from Emma what she knew, and Carl would dispose of her. He would then have a backup in case of disaster with Carl. Perhaps the time was getting very close to doing the impossible. When it was done he could truly disappear. He could finally publish his life's work and get the recognition he deserved. The Nobel prize was a certainty, as soon as he had sanitised the processes by which he had got his results!

CHAPTER 10

LATER THURSDAY CALLUM

Callum had decided that if he was to understand what was happening to him, he would need help, and the only person he completely trusted right now was Emma. With that conclusion in his mind, he got to his feet and started down the hill back towards the village. About halfway down the hill he heard the sound of a two-stroke outboard starting up and curious to see the source of the noise he looked up to see…Emma? Emma was stood up in the back of Iain's boat and was chasing Sammy out of the bay into the Sound of Iona.

"Emmmmmaaaaaa!" shouted Callum even though he knew that there was no chance that Emma would hear him above the noise of the engine. I wonder what she's up to thought Callum and where did she borrow that lifejacket? Callum ran down the rest of the hill and straight across the beach towards the ferry. He could watch where Emma was going from the top of the quay. After the nightmare adventures of the night before Emma had said only this morning that she had had enough of boats for a while.

As Callum approached the ferry that was surging in and out on a series of small waves, its ramp fully down and grating on the concrete of the slipway, he spotted Laura McDowell one of the ferry staff who could normally be found checking tickets as the tourists walked on the ferry. Maybe she had spoken with Emma and knew where she was off to. As he ran up to Laura she looked up from talking with a diminutive customer and spotted Callum. As she did so her mouth fell open (Callum had never actually seen that before, only read about it), she went pale and dropped her ticket stubs that were instantly picked up by the breeze and re-deposited in the sea.

"Ca Ca Ca Call Callum!" she exclaimed.

"Aye, Laura. Ye luk like ye've seen a goost!"

"But I just seen yous goo oot on the boat wi the wee girl Emma".

"What's that yer sayin Laura, I've been up above there!" said Callum pointing back the way he'd just come.

"There's no mistakin what I saw," insisted Laura. "Yon lass came haretailin it doon the slip wi Lottie and got inte Iain's boot. Lottie ran back up the hill and Sammy started larking around and Emma started the boot and took off after Sammy. You's was lyin in the bottom of the boot. Ye didne look well but I put that doon to last neet. I'm telling ya, I knoo what I saw! I guessed that yud had a barney 'cause ye didne speak to the girl at all!"

Callum stood silently his mind racing. "Aye we'd had a row and Emma dropped me off on the other side of the slip. Ye havne seen a goost Laura!"

"Oh aye? An I suppose that ye had time to change yer clothes as well did ya? There's something not reet about this Callum an I'll be talking wi yer Pa as soon as we get back from Iona. If yer comin wi us yu'll need te get on noo!"

Just as Laura stopped speaking the ramp started to lift and without thinking Callum leapt on board. He climbed to the wheelhouse where Seamus was taking the ferry out to begin its fifteen-minute crossing to Iona. On a normal day Callum would have loved to sit in the wheelhouse looking at the brass controls that moved the four multi-directional water jets that powered the ferry. All four jets could be pointed in any direction and this meant that the ferry could go forwards, backwards and even sideways. It always amazed Callum when the ferry turned through 180 degrees within its own body length. Today, however, he was more interested in where Emma had gone.

"Seamus, did ye see Emma in Iain's boot?"

"Ah now I did that Callum." Even after fifteen years on the island Seamus had never lost his native Donegal drawl. "She went away across."

"Did ye see where she landed?" demanded Callum

"She didn't land now, she hitched on to the posh motor cruiser there. Ye see the one getting underway?"

"Aye I see it! How could I not, it must be 15 metres long!"

157

"More like 20 I'd be saying" said Seamus looking across the sound.

"Do ye know whose she is?"

"I do," replied Seamus, "her name is Evolution and she belongs to a Doctor Christian Slack and she berths away across there in Oban."

Callum went cold when he heard the name. He had heard that name Doctor Christian Slack recently. Wasn't that the name of the Doctor who had run the LSD experiments? Wasn't he the one that Emma was trying to track down? Callum didn't know how they'd done it but somehow, they had lured Emma on to that cruiser. Why? Whatever it was it wasn't good news. Not for Emma. First her parents and now her. Emma had been convinced that it was because of him that her parents had been attacked. Maybe they really had been after her all along.

"What are you after doing then?" said Seamus as they ground to a halt on the slipway that was the heart of the tiny village on Iona. It was from this slipway that every visitor to the island got off the ferry or a private boat and wandered around the island. Some visiting for the wildlife and the beaches, most wandering away to their right to see the Abbey and read all about the illustrious history of the island.

"I have absolutely no idea!" shouted Callum over his shoulder as he ran as fast as he could down the three sets of steps onto the ramp and out across the quay. He had seen the Evolution heading along the south side of Iona out towards Staffa (not again thought Callum), He could run as fast as it was going now. As long as they didn't speed up he could keep up with them. He ran up towards the local school and then turned right past the Abbey; he ran for about a mile before looking out to sea again and hopes of catching the cruiser before it passed the end of the island were dashed. The bow had risen, and the wake increased, it was picking up speed. Callum knew that if he was to follow he would have to get height to be able to see it. He turned left on to the footpath that would take him up to the highest point on Iona from where he knew that on a beautiful day like this one he could see for twenty or thirty miles. When he got to the top he had a moment of doubt, was this the right thing to do? If they knew that he could teletransfer mightn't they be expecting this? Callum reviewed what he had seen on his way up the hill as he ran past the Abbey. Who were those two men looking incongruous in their fishing boots tagged on the end of the Abbey tour? He hadn't noticed them before, but they had looked at him intently as he ran past. Maybe he was imagining it or maybe this was a trap. He ran back up to the steep brow of the hill and lying on his belly and looking back over the brow he could see the two men walking at a brisk pace along the road towards the foot of the hill. Callum knew that no Abbey tour came this far. He had maybe ten minutes before they got to him, or to his body. Without thinking too much Callum threw himself down the seaward side of the hill and took off to his left. If he was lucky he could find the small gorse covered cave that he and Andrew had played in for so many hours a few summers ago. He would be able to see out, but unless you knew what you were looking for it was very difficult to find. This was his home, and nobody knew it as well as him!

CHAPTER 11

LATER THURSDAY EMMA

Emma followed Sammy out of the bay and across the sound. Although she was becoming increasingly confident with the boat (who would have thought even three days ago that she would be able to handle a boat), she was also getting increasingly annoyed with Callum for not stopping his silly seal games and sitting up and talking to her. She was still upset by his nasty e-mail to Andrew and she wanted a proper apology.

As they crossed the sound, Emma could see that Sammy (Callum), was clearly heading towards a large motor cruiser called Evolution. She could see the name clearly written on the side of the boat she was heading towards. There were several men on board. One of them seemed to be in charge. He was about 6 foot tall and was quite athletic looking, with black short hair that was receding from the front of his head and was in danger of leaving a little tuft. An isolated outcrop of hair left as the balding tide retreated across the sandy beach of his pate. As Emma got close, she changed her course slightly to follow Sammy around to the other side of the cruiser, the side that was hidden from Fionnphort. As she killed the motor she looked up to see that the man she had seen earlier, also had striking blue eyes, unusual with such dark hair and, now she was within 3 metres of him, she could see he had a dark swarthy complexion.

"Miss Higgins. It is a pleasure to meet you. My name is Doctor Christian Slack."

As he was speaking Emma could feel doubt and fear rising from the depths of her stomach up her gullet and into her mouth.

"And this is…"

Even as he spoke Emma knew. She knew that she had been tricked. She knew that the boy in the boat was not Callum. She should have known. The real Callum would have shown himself, the real Callum would not have worn DECK SHOES. Emma's eyes flickered to the engine starter cord even as another man secured the boat fore and aft to the larger Cruiser.

"No Miss Higgins, you will not be allowed to leave this boat" said the Doctor, and as he spoke a gun appeared in his hand pointing directly towards her.

Although desperately scared, Emma could feel her mind working overtime with thoughts flitting in and out of her head. 'It isn't the gun that kills, it is the person holding the gun. There is nothing intrinsically evil about a gun, it is just an object'. This was an argument that Emma's dad had with her about guns and gun crime, and it was a fine distinction when you were looking down the cold steel muzzle of one thought Emma. Whether or not it was the person or the gun that killed, if she didn't do what she was told she would be just as dead.

"And this is Carl." The Doctor motioned towards the fake Callum who had sat up in Iain's skiff and was smiling at her. He was remarkably similar to Callum but close up she could see that there were subtle differences in the shape of the face and the way that the smile was on his lips but not in his eyes. This was definitely not her Callum. My Callum?

"Yes my dear we are expecting him any time so I would be grateful if you would accompany me downstairs to the stateroom where we will wait for his arrival. I wonder what form he will take? It will be interesting to see how well he has done without any proper training."

"This way," said Carl, as he led Emma out of the boat onto the rear deck of the cruiser, through the wheelhouse and down carpeted steps into the stateroom. Emma was amazed at the voice, apart from having a very posh accent that would be more at home in the grounds of Eton than in the Scottish highlands Carl sounded exactly like his twin. This was less like a boat and more like a hotel, thought Emma but the luxurious surroundings didn't reduce her anxiety and now she was worried about Callum as well. These people knew what he could do, and she had led him into a trap. How could they be sure that they could capture him? If they caught the animal he became wouldn't he just teletransfer into another one and escape? In order to truly capture him, they would have to get his...of course! They were luring him out to the boat to get him away from his body so that it would be vulnerable. They could kill his body and he would never know anything about it. He was clever though. Not as clever as her, but he was clever. Surely he would work out that it was a trap and then not chase her. He would tell his brother and the police would catch them. But would he trust his brother?

"So, my dear. Why don't you tell me what you know?" said the Doctor, while idly tapping the gun against the arm of the white leather chair he had just sunk into.

"No thank you" replied Emma in a dead pan voice.

"No really, I insist" said the Doctor raising the gun to point in her direction. "It is really easy to shoot someone and still have them talk" he added. Emma sneaked a glance at Carl who was lost in his own thoughts.

"Very well then..." Emma took a long breathe and... "I know a lot about a lot of things. I know that this boat is being driven by an inboard diesel engine with a screw propeller which turns. As it turns the water is propelled backwards and that produces a force that pushes the boat forwards. The engine is driven by internal combustion of a hydrocarbon fuel that is mixed with air, which contains oxygen. When it burns, it releases energy and expands this in turn pushes a piston which..."

"Enough of this rubbish! Your friends may be amused by your silly games, but I am not. Now tell me what you know about my activities with regard to teletransference? From your very recent computer use, I know that you have managed to link me to the two buffoons who kidnapped your parents."

Emma tried not to look shocked. How could she have been so stupid as to not run a virus check on her PC after she'd KNOWN that someone had been searching it.

"You hide your feelings well Miss Higgins. Also, Carl my congratulations to you, the worm you created which infected Miss Higgins PC has done its job admirably and has effectively sealed her fate. Now Miss Higgins, tell me what you know of my... ah...activities over the years."

"If you shoot me I will not be able to talk because I will shut down. It happened last year when I fell and hurt my arm. The doctors were frustrated by my inability to speak. You are going to kill me anyway, so why should I tell you what you want to know? There is nothing in it for me. Besides, someone will hear the gun and come and catch you."

"You are a clever and brave girl Miss Higgins"

"Call me Emma"

"...but you aren't quite as clever as you think. Firstly, the gun has a silencer on it so no one on shore will hear me shoot you...and you forget that I am a pharmacologist. I don't rely on crude threats of violence to get what I want." As he spoke the Doctor had risen and walked across to a doctor's bag. He opened the bag and took out two syringes and two vials, both of which contained a clear liquid. Just as Emma had seen a hundred times on the television, the Doctor inserted the tips of the syringes one after the other into the vials. He withdrew a small amount into each syringe and in turn, he turned the syringes upside down, flicked them to make the bubbles rise to the surface, and then ejected a small amount that Emma could see against the light of the porthole.

"You and your friend Callum have annoyed me. You have disrupted my plans and you have forced me to lose two operatives in Oban. Callum I need my dear, but you I don't. One of these contains a serum that will hurt you very much. The other contains a serum that will make you tell me anything I want to know."

"I doubt it," said Emma, sounding braver than she felt. "The skill in using Sodium Pentathol is in asking the questions. My mother could get it out of me, but I doubt whether you could."

"Carl, go and find out if they have found the body of the boy yet and leave me with this annoying child. She will learn not to disrespect the Doctor." This was said in a voice that sent chills down Emma's back. She knew that she did sound brave but that she wasn't. If she believed that there was anything that she could tell this horrible man that would save her then she would.

"Yes Doctor," said Carl who then walked through the stateroom doors and up the steps to the wheelhouse. As he did so, the Doctor followed and closed the doors behind him.

"Best not to be disturbed my dear, I wouldn't want to upset any of my 'employees'. Some of the fools think that women and children deserve to be treated differently!" The Doctor held one of the syringes in his left hand and the gun, that was still pointing at Emma, in his right. He started towards her seeing the fear in her eyes. "First my dear, I will make you hurt. How a person responds to extreme pain is always scientifically interesting. Then I will make you talk. You see I really need to know how much you have worked out. It will affect the timing of our plans. What my dear? You look surprised? Did you think that I would not go through with my threats?"

"I was sure that you would go through with your threat. What surprises me, is to see a monkey about to inject you!" replied Emma.

As she spoke, the Doctor spun around in time to see a much more agile monkey step to one side and stab the other syringe into his gluteus maximus, the large muscle in his bottom. He staggered forward across the room, hitting his shins on the coffee table and collapsing into the chair on the opposite side of the room.

"Callum?"

The monkey made monkey noises and jumped onto Emma's lap.

"You must go back to your body, they are looking for you!" said Emma urgently. The monkey nodded but stayed.

"Can we get out back the way you came?" again, the monkey nodded.

"Look, there's a talking monkey!" This was said in a sing-song voice by a now drunk looking Doctor who had remained seated. He was holding the syringe that he had just pulled from his own backside. "Those nasty little children injected me in the arse!" he said, although to whom he was directing his remarks was distinctly unclear. While Emma was gazing at the Doctor who did not seem to be himself, she became aware of a banging on the now locked door.

"Doctor, the fools have not yet found his body and the eagle has been let out of its cage! Doctor! The boy Callum must be here! Doctor!"

"It's OK," said the Doctor in a voice that would never be heard outside the door where the engine would be roaring. "He's in here with me, and he's a monkey!" With this the Doctor burst into a fit of giggles and slumped down in the chair.

"Callum we must go," Emma said urgently.

Callum jumped down and held up his hand for Emma to take and scooted towards the door that led down into the rest of the ship. Just as he got there, he stopped and dragged Emma back in front of the Doctor. What was he doing?

"Callum?"

Callum jumped up onto the coffee table where there was a pen and some papers. He grabbed a pen in his monkey paw and wrote for less than a second. Emma looked at the paper.

It was a question mark! Callum wanted her to ask the Doctor questions. But what questions?

"What are you doing here?"

As she asked the question there was an almighty crash on the door as if some large person had thrown their shoulder against it. Emma wasn't sure, but she thought that she had heard a groan and the door hadn't given at all. She said a silent 'thank you' to the makers of such a sturdy boat.

"I am being questioned by a silly little girl whose hair is so short she looks like a boy" giggled the Doctor.

Oh no thought Emma. No one beats me at that game!

167

"Doctor, earlier you said that you had plans that could be affected. What is the nature of those plans?"

As she asked the question there was another crash against the door and this time they could see the point of the axe as it pierced the fine oak of the door.

"Our plans to be powerful and rich of course!"

She had to be specific! She should know that of all people!

"Who are you going to kill?"

Another crash had splintered enough for an arm to come poking through with a gun at the end of it pointing in her direction. After a second the arm withdrew, presumably because they were scared of hitting the Doctor.

"Kill? The little girlie wants to know who we are going to kill. Kill my dear? Why nobody…ha ha ha ha…"

The Doctor was looking more ill and was slurring his words now so much that they were difficult to understand.

Another crash and they could clearly see daylight streaming through the smashed door.

"What are you going to steal?"

"Who's a clever little girl. I'm going to steal a nuclear warhead my dear!"

Crash!

"Callum, let's go!" Emma urged and tried to drag him out of the stateroom. The monkey was surprisingly strong and had a pleading look in his eyes as they gazed into hers. "What?" Emma gazed into Callum's eyes and suddenly she knew what he wanted to ask. The Doctor knew all about teletransference, he had adopted Callum's twin brother and it was him that did the tests with LSD on the soldiers years before. He had to know.

But what could she ask him? She had to be specific! It was a gamble, she only had time for one more question!

"Why did you have Callum's mother killed?"

She could feel the monkey tense, she could hear the door finally splintering and time seemed to slow right down.

"I didn't want to, but she questioned me! I loved her you know. She said the testing should stop...she was very beautiful. When she tried to leave with the twins I had to stop her!" The giggle had gone from the Doctor's face and his voice was tinged with sadness.

A final mighty crash broke the moment and two men burst through the door. Emma ran straight down the corridor. She stepped over a snake that had a still wriggling mouse halfway into its mouth and skirted a very angry otter. She saw the monkey who was much faster than her, scoot past and lead her towards an open porthole at the end of the corridor. Emma guessed that this was where Callum had got in. The monkey stood to its full height and pantomimed diving in and going deep. She started to climb into the porthole when she caught a glimpse of the first man at the end of the corridor. He was running with something held out in front of him. It was a gun. As Emma started to topple backwards through the open window, she just had time to see the monkey jump straight up in front of her, blocking her from the view of the gunman. She marvelled at how like humans monkeys were. She marvelled at how their physiology was so similar, about how 96% of their DNA was the same as humans. She marvelled at how when she heard the gun go off she could see the monkey's chest depress just where the bullet had hit it and she marvelled as she toppled backwards into the sea at how she knew that the bullet had gone straight through the monkey's heart and how she knew that the monkey was dead.

CHAPTER 12

LATER THURSDAY CALLUM

Having found his hideaway, Callum relaxed and started to look out towards where he could see Evolution motoring out towards Staffa and the open sea. The Evolution was a magnificent creation. About as long as two of the coaches that delivered tourists to Fionnphort. It was on three levels with an open cockpit above what must be the stateroom with three windows and then towards the front of the long sleek bows were portholes... one of which was open. He needed to get there, and he needed to get there fast. Flying was going to be quickest. A herring gull was close, so for the second time he searched for the gull in his mind, found it and determined to be the gull. The usual nausea was just a minor irritation now and he was quickly flying along driving the gull towards the yacht. As he got closer, he relaxed his hold on the gull and allowed it to wheel and call along with the other gulls over the boat. He noticed that the gulls would often swoop down and perch on the front of the boat. Callum swooped down and displacing the gull that was already there sat on the handrail some 15 metres from the boy that had obviously tricked Emma. Callum could see why. It was almost like looking in a mirror. Where had they found this look-alike? How much trouble had they gone to, to create a facsimile of him, and more importantly; why?

This was not the time to wonder on such imponderables but time to find Emma and get her off this boat.

The first thing he had to do was organise a rescue and for that he would need something big and powerful. Callum let his mind wander through the waters surrounding the boat and he found lots of choices. His ability to teletransfer into an animal certainly had a range but it had grown and grown in the few days since he had discovered this ability, and he found he could sense the minds of a great many creatures for a long way around the boat and there were about twenty seals in… in what? Not in sight, not in earshot, in…"telerange"? Telerange, that will do. There were loads of seals in telerange and a medium size one would do, but he had to get to Emma in time. Callum waited until the look-alike was facing the back of the boat gazing out back towards Iona and where he had left his body. He knew that he should be feeling the tug, the pull of his body on his mind but he could still see the hillside where it lay, and he could imagine that he could see the hollow under the heather where it was hidden.

Callum took off, circled the boat and flew straight through the open porthole at the front of the boat. As soon as he was inside he realised how awful his gull body was in this situation. He quickly let his mind search, and he found a cluster of creatures really close by. Intrigued, he pecked against the nearest door. It swung open and he was amazed to see a medium-sized room full of cages and tanks and aquaria, in turn full of all sorts of creatures from a mouse to snake, otter, eagle, cockroach and others. The monkey would be best for its opposable thumbs. He quickly transferred and let as many creatures out as he could with his clever monkey hands. At one point, he thought the eagle was going to have a go at him but the gull wanted to get out of the boat and the eagle followed it gratefully to the porthole. The eagle flapped on the sill and Callum realised that as soon as it appeared they would know that he was here. He ran down the length of the corridor and silently opened the door in to the stateroom locking it behind him. What he saw there filled him with dread. A large man in his fifties advancing on Emma, who looked really scared, with a syringe in his hand. Callum's first thought was to look around the room for a weapon that a small monkey could use to whack this guy over the head. As he did so, he spotted a second syringe that was obviously full. Without thinking he picked it up ran to the man and stuck it into his behind.

It was great to see Emma still alive and apparently undamaged. He was so happy to see her that a little part of the monkey broke through and without planning to he jumped into her lap where she absentmindedly stroked him. It was quite nice.

After a few minutes and asking the guy (who turned out to be Doctor Christian Slack) some questions during which he discovered that he had a twin and that his real mother was dead, murdered by Doctor Slack, it was time to run. Emma ran down towards the porthole and Callum was already searching with his mind for a seal. As he ran past Emma and showed her that she needed to dive deep to avoid the screws of the boat and any gunfire, he found a likely candidate within a hundred metres of the boat. Just as he was about to transfer he saw a man running toward them with a gun in his hand. Without thinking, he jumped straight up between the man and Emma and transferred. He hoped the monkey would be OK, why would they shoot the monkey? They would know that Callum had been in it, and it was Callum that had caused all the trouble.

As soon as Callum was in the head of the seal, he could sense a commotion in the water about fifty metres away. He turned and swam as fast as he could to the source of the noises and he could clearly see Emma hanging in the water about 5 metres below the boat. The boat had gone past Emma, but the men on board were shooting at her. Callum could see the paths of the bullets as they ripped through the water and Emma was clearly still in danger. Callum swam up to Emma and nudged her. He could see the relief on her face and he turned so that she could wrap her arms around him and just using his tail he dived a little deeper and took off towards the shore. Almost immediately he could feel her pulling up on his flippers and it dawned on him that a seal could stay under water for 20 minutes but that a human couldn't! He decided that they were a long way away from the boat by now, so he risked surfacing. He could hear Emma sobbing for breath and he could see the Evolution roaring towards them and even in this dire situation he marvelled at the turning circle of such a fabulous boat. He could probably stay out of its way, but he wouldn't be able to outrun it and when they went ashore the boat would be only seconds behind them. They had to stop that boat. Callum had an idea. It was dangerous, and he wished he could discuss it with Emma but with seconds to decide he had to act. He dived again with Emma clinging on for dear life, and he swam toward the gap between Iona and Eilean Annraidh. It would have been clear to whoever was following them that they were running from the boat and heading for the beach on the north side of Iona to land. Callum surfaced often and the boat was gaining on them. He felt a few bullets enter the water to either side of them and then he saw what he was looking for in front of him. The bottom that had been sandy and about 15 metres down suddenly flew towards them and he was skimming between sharp rocks only centimetres below the surface, their presence hidden from a casual observer by the ruffled surface caused by a light wind. Then they were through and the bottom returned to 15 metres down and sandy. Callum risked surfacing one more time to make sure that the boat could see where they had gone and then he dived and doubled back. Back towards the tip of the island where he had left his body. As he turned, he could hear an almighty crash, the screaming of engines that had lost their propellers and a great shudder through the water. The Evolution had fallen for it and had hit the rocks at 25 knots. The bottom had been ripped out of her and she would be sinking fast. That will have been the costliest shipwreck in these seas for many a year.

Callum stayed under until Emma was pulling on his flippers really hard and then he risked a quick surface. The Evolution was nowhere to be seen and everyone who had been on the yacht was too busy looking after themselves and the Doctor to worry about them. Callum could see them all swimming towards the nearest beach on the north west of Iona or clinging to floating wreckage of the Evolution. Callum just hoped that none of the animals that were on the yacht were hurt. He really couldn't care less about Slack or his long-lost twin. After a few minutes, he became aware of Emma holding on to his back and shivering. It hadn't occurred to him, him being a seal, that the water was cold. He turned away from the carnage in the water and completed the journey to the beach on the south side of the island. Emma crawled out of the sea and collapsed on the beach. There was nothing he could do for her here so he concentrated on his own body and...

He found himself back in his own body and suddenly a wave of exhaustion swept over him. Three big transfers after last nights' exertions had taken it out of him and he knew he needed to rest. But first he needed to find Emma down on the beach below him. He stood up and instantly regretted it. He could see the two men that had been tracking him about 100 metres away. They were looking right at the place he had hidden his body. Rats! Callum dropped out of sight, but he knew that they had clocked his position. He thought he could outrun them, even as exhausted as he was but he wouldn't be able to outrun them forever and he needed to get down the hill to find Emma. What he really needed was for them to leave of their own accord. They must have seen the Evolution sink, Callum wondered why they hadn't gone to help? Perhaps they had received orders to stay up here waiting for Callum to return. Callum didn't want to think what those orders would be.

There was nothing else for it. One more transfer. For the fourth time that day Callum searched with his mind to find a creature that would be fast enough, scary enough, and big enough to scare off two grown men who were probably armed. He also needed it to be here quickly as the men were closing in. That was it, a buzzard…no there …a bit further away but exactly what he wanted. The sheep dog at the farm he had passed earlier. Callum concentrated and as soon as he was in, he ran as fast as he could until the rope that the sheep dog was tied up with snapped taught on his neck. He turned and ran back to the ring in the wall and with his human brain, he found it easy to untie the rope that was thankfully only looped through his collar and then he was off. The speed that a determined sheep dog can reach, even uphill, astounded Callum and it seemed like only moments before he was sneaking up on the two men who were only metres away from his body. He lowered himself down on his haunches and was just about to sink his dangerously sharp (no wonder he had been tied up) canines into a human leg when he heard a strange squawking that grabbed the attention of the two men. The taller of the two men took a radio off his belt and pressed a button "Aye."

"Have you got him?" It was his twin. It sounded remarkably like him, just with a slightly nasal English accent.

"We'll ha im in just a wee minute. He's aroond here sumwhere. We saw him a couple a minutes since."

"There is a change of orders. When you find him. Kill him."

"Hang on a wee minute, I neva signed up te murder."

"You signed up to carry out my orders. If you don't want to carry out my orders, I will see to it that your fishing quota is revoked and your boat impounded. How will you feed your pretty little daughter? The one who could easily be picked up from school in Oban."

The dog that Callum currently occupied could sense the menace in the voice and could feel the fear in the fisherman. Why did they fear a 12 year old?

"I'd like to speak wi the Doctor"

"The Doctor is not available to speak with anyone at the moment, so you take your orders from me, NOW CARRY THEM OUT!"

The radio went dead to silence from the two men who were looking at each other with a mixture of fear and apprehension on their faces.

"Angus, this is not fer me" said the short man.

"Will, we've been together for fifteen years on the boot, ye'll not leave me to do this alone."

"Aye man I will. I'm reet sorry Angus but I'm no in fer this" and with that the man walked off back down the hill towards the farm.

The taller man, Angus looked for a second as if he would follow but then hesitated.

Now! Thought Callum. The man needs some encouragement to leave and he erupted from the heather a biting snarling ball of black and white fury. He had got three good bites in before the man had really comprehended what was happening. Callum caught his breath and the man took his opportunity to drop the radio, turn and run after his mate.

And don't come back! Thought Callum.

Callum quickly transferred back into his own body and started off down the hill to find Emma, very aware that the search for Emma was almost certainly still ongoing by his twin and his men. After another ten minutes he got to the beach where he had left Emma to find no sign of her. Even the place where she had crawled out of the sea had by this time been covered by the tide.

Callum staggered back up to the head of the beach and collapsed on the grass. He was exhausted. Too many transfers in not enough time. If he just had the energy for one more, he could find her easily with the help of a gull. Just then it dawned on him that if he could teletransfer then so could his twin! That was why there were so many different animals on the yacht. That was how the Doctor knew what he could do! That was why he HAD TO GET OUT OF SIGHT! If he could teletransfer into a gull, then so could his twin!

Callum scrambled to his feet and ran towards the rocks to the north of the beach where he knew there were some small shallow caves. He got there and fell again onto the sand out of sight from the air.

"Hello" said Emma, who was sitting right at the back of the cave. "I wondered how long it would take you to figure it out. You don't look very well you know."

"Aye well neither would ye if ye'd done all that I have today!" snapped Callum.

"I haven't had a very nice time either, you know".

"No. I suppose not," admitted Callum grudgingly.

"Also, I've been thinking," said Emma "there was a cockroach in my hair when I crawled out of the sea. It scuttled away into a crevice in a rock. It's still there."

"I'm really tired Emma, if yer waitin on me to leap to a conclusion ye'll have a long wait."

"Sorry. I think that Carl was in the cockroach when we were in the stateroom, but I think that he went back to his body when I jumped off the ship. If he'd still been with us when we came ashore-re-re he would have fou-nd-nd us."

"Aye lass and yer freezing cold. You'll have to keep yer troosers but ye can wear my jumper."

Callum turned his back while Emma gratefully took his jumper. She stripped to the waist and pulled the jumper over her head. As soon as it was clear that she was decent, Callum stood up again and walked towards her. He held out his hand and she stood up. Callum then sat down without a word where Emma had been and pulled her down to sit on his knee with her back to his front and his arms around her. Emma tensed immediately, "what are you doing?"

"Don't panic lass I'm just sharing the body heat. You'll get warmer quicker like this than any other way. Just relax, ye know I'm a gentleman."

Emma relaxed and said, "If they can't find us quickly, they will have to get on with their plan immediately you know. They will try to steal the nuclear warhead tonight or maybe tomorrow and I think I know where from. There is only one nuclear establishment anywhere near here. It is the submarine base at Faslane in Gare Loch, north west of Glasgow. It is about 100 miles from here, but the wildlife will be the same. That's why they had the animals. They will be using Carl's teletransferring skills to get in through the security and to get the warhead out…although nothing they had on the boat would get a warhead out. We must get back as soon as you think the coast is clear and warn the Ministry of Defence… but hold on, the Ministry is covering up for the Doctor. What if they are behind stealing the warhead themselves? Callum this isn't making any sense…Callum…"

Emma turned her head, but still couldn't see Callum with his face pressed sideways on to her back. She couldn't see him, but she could feel the rhythmic breathing and she could hear the gentle snoring. After the night he'd had and the number of transfers he had done today, she wasn't surprised he was asleep. Perhaps she would give him an hour and then they would need to get back to warn someone. She eased herself away from Callum and encouraged him to lie down on the sand where the sun was still shining, albeit weakly, and she lay down in front of him and wrapped his arms around her to keep warm. She lay there trying to judge time thinking that it was quite nice having Callum's arms around her like this. Even when she was very small she didn't like being hugged and cuddled but this felt different. This was quite nice.

They were found, still fast asleep, by the search party headed up by Angus Green six hours later, at exactly 11.33 pm.

Chapter 13

Overnight Thursday

"Callum McBride! What do ye think yer doin?"

Callum and Emma woke with a start, cold in the late evening glow.

"Angus. What are ye doing here?" asked Callum.

"First of all, my name to ye is Constable Green ye wee…and secondly, I'm here looking for yous pair! Yer ma is frantic missy, and I've got Laura McDowell saying there were two Callums, and I've got a yacht going aground and sinkin, and I've got the Sea King taking sick people off te Oban and last thing I needed were two young uns off for hanky panky on a beach! Now are yous OK?"

"Aye Angus we're fine" said Callum. "I'll have you know that there was no hanky panky, we just fell asleep on the beach. Nay harm done, and no crime committed?"

"Aye well, I suppose we'd better get yous both home. Yer ma is throwin' a wobbly back there missy. We had a report that you'd met up wi the yacht that sank and then Iain's boat was found driftin. Ye've gi us all a scare alreet! The whole village is oot looking for yous. Wait here a moment and I'll call them off." With that he strode off up the hill trying to get reception on his police radio.

"Callum. You must warn him about the warhead. He can speak to the submarine base and warn them to be on the lookout."

"On the lookout for what? For an otter?" Callum picked up an imaginary telephone and spoke in to it. "Hello, can I speak wi the submarine base please. Aye I'll hold. Yes, hello? Is that the commander of the submarine base? It is? Aye well it's Callum McBride here. Aye I'm twelve and I'd like you to be on the lookout for a wee otter. Aye it's really my evil twin brother who I met for the first time today when he ordered his henchmen to kill me. Aye he wants to steal a warhead. What for you say? No idea actually…"

"There is no need to be horrible Callum. I will tell them then. I never lie. They will believe me."

Emma said this with such conviction that for a moment Callum thought that perhaps they might! He turned to Emma and took her hands in his. He looked her straight in the eye and said, "I would believe you Emma, but they won't. Trust me we can't tell anyone."

"What about Iain. He's in MI6 perhaps he will believe you?"

"Aye Emma, Iain would believe me alreet but I'm scared he already knows. He told me his mission was me. He said his mission was to protect me, but he hasn't done a very good job so far. He knew what I could do. He knew before I did. He must have known aboot my real mother and aboot Doctor Slack and mebbe even Carl, but he told me nothing! I cannae trust him."

"Come on you twos!" The call was from Constable Green, so they walked up towards him and back on the path that would take them to Iona village and the ferry crossing back to Fionnphort. For the first few hundred yards they walked in silence, then Callum thought to ask, "Constable Green?"

"Aye lad?"

"What happened to the crew of the Evolution?"

"So you know its name then do ye Callum?" said Constable Green "Is there anything else that ye know that you'd like to get off your chest? I'll get it all oot of ye in the end."

"There's nowt to get, but I was wonderin aboot the crew."

"Well there's no harm in telling you. They were picked up by the Venus back from a fishing trip and four went by ambulance to be checked oot at Salen and two of them went te Oban by Helicopter."

"Why were they teken by helicopter?" demanded Callum.

"The one man must have had a wee bang te the heed. He was talking aboot a monkey and nae mekkin sense at all. The other wee chap…he'd be aboot your age I reckon… had his heed all covered in bandages and wouldnae let anyone look at him. We all thought that the hospital at Oban was the place for the pair of them."

As they were talking, they had met up with two others from the search party that had travelled to Iona to look for Callum and Emma, and Constable Green started talking to them. Every couple of minutes he would turn around and look at Callum or Emma shake his head and go back to talking with the other two volunteers. One of the volunteers was Laura from the ferry and she kept giving Callum some very strange looks.

"Callum" said Emma in an urgent whisper. "What are we going to do? We can't just let the Doctor steal a nuclear warhead! What would he want it for?"

"I don't know," Callum replied trying to keep his voice as low as possible. "I would guess that it is a bargaining chip, a 'get out of jail free card', or mebbe he's going te sell it to terrorists."

"What are we going to do to stop him?" asked Emma again.

"I don't know. I don't know who to tell. Our parents would never believe us and I don't know who to trust in the police or in MI6. You were the one who told me that the MoD put a hold on investigations into Slack by the police. We know that Slack had been watching me for years and he must have at least one spy in the village. Is it coincidence that my brother turns up, apparently working for MI6 the day after I learn what I can do? I don't know who to trust and who to tell, or who would believe me!"

"But the Doctor is already in Oban! It was him on the helicopter with Carl. All they would need to do would be to discharge themselves from Oban hospital and they would be free to steal the warhead."

"You're forgetting that the warhead will be protected with security, the like of which we've never seen!"

"Yes Callum, but if you wanted to get in somewhere, get through a fence, over a wall, walk past a guard without them taking any notice, could you?"

Callum didn't answer but it was perfectly clear to both of them that if he wanted to…he could.

As they approached the ferry slip, Callum could see the scale of the uproar they had caused. There must have been 100 or so people waiting on the slipway for them including the Professor and Mrs Higgins. The Professor was in a wheelchair with his legs sticking out wearing his Jodhpurs again and a Deerstalker hat. Morag was there. Seamus was there. Even the ferry itself was there! It had normally been put away by this time in its overnight birth in Bull Hole, and up in the wheelhouse was Mr McBride looking like thunder. As they got to the crowd it parted which allowed Mrs Higgins to run to Emma.

"Oh Angel, where have you been? We were so worried about you!"

Emma was engulfed in hugs and stood there enduring them while the crowd started to get on board the ferry. "Callum!"

"Aye Mrs Higgins?"

"I think that you and Emma should spend a little bit of time apart dear. I think it's all getting too much."

Callum looked at Mrs Higgins and again at Emma. Maybe she was right. Their whole family had been put in mortal peril by knowing Callum. It was Callum who had this ability, it was Callum who had the twin, and it was Callum whose brother was in MI6. Maybe he should stop seeing Emma, at least that way she wouldn't get into any more trouble.

"Aye Mrs Higgins, perhaps yer reet."

Emma threw Callum an extremely unhappy look as Mrs Higgins led her back to Professor Higgins who was sitting looking pompous at the other side of the ferry. Some of the islanders were still looking at him and his outrageous garb and muttering to themselves.

"Callum. Yer da would like yer to come up to the wheelhoose!"

It was Seamus on the foot of the steps beckoning to him. Callum wasn't looking forward to this conversation, so he started up the steps slowly and heard Emma call out from below;

"Callum!" he turned to look at her, "keep your mobile on!"

How did she know he had a mobile? He never used it at home as the reception wasn't great and he couldn't afford the calls. It had been a present from Iain the previous Christmas. It had been so that he could keep in touch with Mr and Mrs McBride while he was at school. After a few days, he had lost interest and as he couldn't be bothered to phone his school friends who he saw all day and every day at school, he hadn't had much use for it. Maybe he had mentioned it while they had been talking. He shrugged and looked back at Emma who was still looking up at him.

"OK!" he shouted back above the roar of the ferry engines feeling self-conscious that everyone was listening in.

"Callum!" WHAT did she want now? This was getting embarrassing. He considered ignoring her but looked back anyway.

"If Slack can do it so can you!"

Callum wasn't entirely sure he had heard her correctly and even if he had he had no idea what she meant.

As he walked into the wheelhouse Seamus followed him in and stood behind him leaning against the wall.

"Thank you Seamus," came the deep gravely voice. "I'd like a few words alone wi the young un."

Seamus looked far from happy as he left the wheelhouse, but he did as he was asked. Callum just stood looking out of the wheelhouse windows at the slipway in Fionnphort which was fast approaching. His dad looked at him and resumed his duties as pilot. The silence stretched and Callum was feeling really uncomfortable. If he was going to get a big telling off it would have to be soon, or they would be there.

"Callum," here it came. "I don't know exactly what's goin on here wi you and the lass. I'm nae goin to ask fer details, an I'll keep yer ma from yer throat, but I'm countin on yer Callum. I'm countin on yer to do the reet thing."

What did that mean? Thought Callum. His dad had always been a man of few words. 'Enigmatic' Isla had called him. 'Taciturn' Iain had called him.

"Toneet Callum", uh oh, there was more. "Ye dinae do the reet thing. Getting all these nice folks to look for yer wasnae the reet thing."

And that was it. The rollicking he had expected never materialised and his pa docked the ferry, let everyone off and then gently reversed the ferry off the slip and motored out to its overnight mooring. As Callum walked up the quay, trying to do as Mrs Higgins asked and keep away from Emma, he saw Iain waiting for him at the top of the slipway.

"Ye've done well Boat Boy," said Iain ruffling Callum's hair.

"Aye."

"I'm reet sorry that Emma got tricked. After yer dealins the neet before I thought that they would lay low fer a while. We've been clearing up their distribution routes to Spain and from there back to London. Ye've helped to stop a large network of LSD manufacturers and distribution but we're no nearer to finding oot what Slack has really been up tae."

Callum looked up at his 27 year old brother...although not really his brother...and made a decision. He was 12 years old and was deeply, deeply tired. He had information that could prevent the horrific deaths of tens of thousands of people and he had to do something to stop those deaths, to stop that warhead falling into the wrong hands. His dad had told him that he was counting on him to do the 'reet thing', but how could he do the reet thing on his own? It was the only choice he had.

"Iain, I need to talk to ye aboot Slack and what ye do, but ay'm telling yous that I dinae knoo if I can trust ye. Tell me how you got involved wi all of this."

The two adoptive brothers walked onto the beach, lit by the stars with the backdrop of the Abbey on the island of Iona only a short kilometre away across the Sound of Iona to site, to the broken boulder that only the night before had been where Callum had lain whilst searching in Lottie for Mr and Mrs Higgins. Had it really only been 24 hours?

"I joined the poliss out of university 5 years ago, and

at that time I was approached by MI6. We are like a secret poliss force. We deal with terrorists and foreign powers and we keep an eye on lots of things that worry us about security, including drug trafficking. We had been following a number of leads that have led us te Iona for 15 years, rumours about kidnappings, drugs, and drug testing. There was a Lyndsay Smith who turned up in Glasgee with stories of runaway girls being kidnapped in London and dragged away to Scotland for drug testing, we have traced a drugs operation back to an LSD manufacturing plant on Iona that will be raided in the next few days and we have been following the legal battle between the government and the soldiers claims of teletransference. There was a French girl who claimed to be able to teletransfer but she died in an accident a couple of years ago."

"Aye, I know, but I'm no so sure it was an accident" replied Callum. Iain's eyebrows shot up, but he continued his story.

"When I joined the poliss, MI6 were not getting anywhere with their investigations, mainly because the local poliss wer no very helpful and they didnae know the islands at all. So they recruited me. I still draw my pay from the poliss but I'm on secondment to MI6, so although I work as a polissman in Glasgow I am working for MI6 at the same time. I have been following the whereabouts and the activities of Doctor Slack. I know he is tied up in the drugs, and I know he has a blond 12 year old who lives with him. I have seen him myself Callum, I know ye have a twin. The question is, what are they up to?"

Callum listened intently to his brother's story, all of which made perfect sense. Perfect sense, but with great big holes still in the story, things that didn't quite add up. Why had the MoD let Slack take over the LSD manufacturing plant? Why had they put a stop on police investigations into Slack? Why had Iain not simply arrested Slack earlier in the day? Callum had heard Slack talk about his spies in the village and in the Police and in the MoD. Couldn't Iain account for at least two of those?

Callum was tired, confused, and scared but he had to do something. Emma was certain Slack and Carl would try to steal the nuclear warhead from the submarine base at Gare Loch. Assuming that they would wait for Slack to recover from his truth serum injection, the first time they could reasonably be expected to do that would be tomorrow and probably tomorrow night…and what had Emma said as she was walking away…if Slack can do it so can you?

"Iain?"

"Aye Callum?"

"Who else knows aboot me bein able to teletransfer?"

"Just me lad, no one else would ever believe it. I worked it oot mysen after putting it together wi the soldier's stories".

Really? thought Callum. You knew I had a twin, you're only assignment is me but you're never there when I need you, and you believed without question that I could teletransfer?

If Callum was going to stop Slack and Carl stealing a nuclear weapon, he was going to have to do it alone.

Chapter 14

Friday

Callum awoke in his own bed early on Friday morning to a vibrating noise under his pillow. He woke up slowly, slightly bemused as to what it could be. As his consciousness struggled to drag itself, kicking and screaming into the new day, he remembered getting home well after midnight, stumbling upstairs and collapsing into bed, but not before he had plugged in his mobile and turned it on.

Callum scrabbled around and found the source of the vibration. He unplugged it and saw that he had a text.

Slack n C left Ob Hosp 8am. E

He didn't recognise the number but guessed it could only be from Emma. How did she get his number? He had certainly never given it to her. Yet more hacking into databases he supposed. He smiled…that girl was incorrigible! He hoped that she wouldn't get into trouble with all of this.

He hit the reply button and started to send a text

Hor u knnw? D

He hit the send button before he checked the message and in seconds got a reply:

What are you talking about? E

She could obviously text at the same impressive speed she could type. Callum could tie a fishing hook in seconds, but he didn't have the thumbs of an all in wrestler like so many of his classmates from the classic two-thumb messaging.

Callum hit reply again and then decided it would be far simpler to call.

"Emma?"

"Yes?"

"It's me Callum"

"Yes I know, it is your voice from your number."

Callum sighed, he was getting used to it, but this girl could take him from calm to grumpy in one sentence! "Aye alreet, what are we going to do?"

"Have you told your brother?"

"No, I wasnae sure when I spoke with him last night."

"Good, I'm not sure about him either and Callum?"

"Aye?"

"I think I may have found your mum."

Callum felt numb. He was torn between a desire to know and a desire to remain in ignorance. He already knew his mother had been murdered. He already knew that his twin brother had ordered him murdered. How much more did he want to know about his real biological family?

"Will it keep?" he asked Emma tersely,

"Yes. It will keep. I will e-mail it to you."

"Thanks Emma, now what are we going to do?"

"I have been thinking about it, and I think you need to tell your brother."

"I thought we weren't sure about him?" Callum asked with growing incredulity.

"Follow me with this one Callum," said Emma patronisingly, "if he is for real we will need his help, yes?"

"Aye."

"And he is our only source of help because no one else would believe you?"

"Aye"

"Well yesterday on the yacht Slack told me that he had a need for you but not for me...so he must be thinking of using you if anything happened to Carl, right?"

"Aye. Ok"

"If Iain is working with Slack then he will take you straight to him and you can think of a way of messing up his plans. If Iain is on our side, then he will be there to help and if he isn't then you will know for certain."

A silence grew on the phone between Emma and Callum until Emma, fearing that the connection had been lost said

"Callum...are you there?"

"Aye, I'm here. Is that it?"

"Sorry?"

"I thought you were a child genius...and all you've got is 'trust your brother because if he's on your side it will be great and if he isn't he'll take you to the people who have ordered you murdered and then at least you'll know?"

"I know it's not much, Callum. I'm sorry but there isn't anything else. I will do my best to find some evidence to link Slack to the drugs and warhead online, but I think it is up to you. Sorry."

And with that she was gone.

Callum had barely begun to think things through before a knock came at the door.

"Callum." It was Iain, "We need to go."

"Where?" shouted Callum as he pulled a t-shirt over his head.

"The mainland. Slack has skipped from Oban Hospital, he had a police guard, but they were attacked by a cat of all things, I'm guessing that was your twin, this morning and while they were trying to catch it he and the boy skipped. We are attempting to track them but Callum, no one would believe me if I told them that the cat was Carl. I might need your help."

Callum was torn. "No one would believe me if I told them"…that was what Iain had said and it was a mightily convenient cover if you wanted to keep who you really worked for secret. But if that was true, how could Callum be Iain's assignment? Someone would have to know in order to give Iain his assignment. Something didn't feel right but the words of his father were still in his ears from the previous evening"…but I'm countin on yer Callum. I'm countin on yer to do the reet thing." He was who he was. He couldn't think of another option to do the "reet" thing…and after all he needed to know if his brother was on his side or not.

"Gi me two minutes. I'll be reet there." Callum shouted to his supposedly MI6 brother.

195

One thing about going with his brother was that it was very exciting. Iain and Callum grabbed a bite to eat, were waved off by Mrs McBride, and by 9.30 am were high above Fionnphort in an army helicopter flying across to Oban on the mainland. Whether or not Iain actually was in MI6, he certainly had contacts in high places to be able to commandeer an army helicopter at such short notice, and then to be able to bring his little brother along for the ride. Callum was impressed whoever's side Iain was on.

"We'll get to Oban and then track south by road", he had said to Callum as they got on in the Columba centre carpark. Callum had looked across to the new front door of Emma's house but saw no one stirring. "We will wait until our operatives get some trace and then we'll move in. I have two teams from Glasgee on standby. Whatever it is he is up to we'll catch him red handed."

"Is it not possible he's just running away?" Callum had asked.

"Aye lad, it's possible" Iain had replied thoughtfully, "but why would you need a lad who has been trained to teletransfer, just to run away? No, I think there is something going on, and I mean to find out what!"

Unless you already know, thought Callum.

The helicopter only took twenty minutes to get to Oban, a journey that usually took Callum three hours on his way to school. His school friends would be amazed if they could see him now. It seemed faintly ridiculous that it was less than a week since he'd been at school in Oban so looking forward to the summer holidays. In a moment of prescience, Callum somehow doubted that he would be going back to that school again.

They were met by a fast, sleek BMW 5 series unmarked police car, and Karen, the policewoman that had questioned Callum and Emma two days previously was behind the wheel.

"Hi Callum"

"Hi"

"Iain, is it safe for Callum to be along?"

So, she knew Iain well then.

"We havne a choice, Callum and Emma are important to Slack so he's important to us too. Now drive. South". Did Karen know? Callum's head was spinning. This wasn't like a book, he couldn't just stay up late reading with a torch under his covers to see how it all ended! Besides, in the books he'd read it always ended well for the hero. Was he the hero? Maybe everyone is their own hero and it doesn't end well for everyone. Look at his real mum, she was the heroine in her story and it didn't end well for her. Maybe this story wouldn't end well for him. Maybe if someone was reading this in a book they'd get halfway through the final chapter and he'd be killed and the rest of the pages would be blank…

Karen drove the BMW smoothly away from the helipad and took the main road to Glasgow out of Oban via Craignure.

As the car sped along the main road, often being slowed by caravans, it passed the turning on the right to Inverary and without thinking, Callum blurted out "We're going the wrong way!"

Iain looked at him with a quizzical look.

"I mean wi the caravans at this time of year, would it no be quicker down the other side?"

"He's reet. Let's go down through Inverary."

"Ok, you're the boss," said Karen as she did a U-turn in front of a caravan towing 4x4 that beeped its horn at them.

Again, Iain turned to look at Callum and gave him a quizzical look.

Callum studiously ignored his brother and looked out of the window. This way would shave a few minutes off their run to Gare Loch and Her Majesty's Naval Base Clyde, also known as Faslane, the home of the UK's submarine based nuclear deterrent. Surely that was where Slack and Carl would steal the warhead.

About ten minutes into the journey Callum was awoken for the second time that day by vibrations of his Nokia mobile going off. It was actually an Iain cast-off and he surreptitiously unlocked the phone while Karen and Iain were deep in conversation in the front of the car and read his message from Emma.

What's happening? E

Driving from Oban to Faslane Chasing Doctor S Karen WPC in car. Who is she?

Wanted to wave this morning. Saw u in chopper. Will check out K. Keep me informed.

'Keep me informed?' Who did she think she was? Still, it was nice to know that she was out there thinking of him. He still didn't know whether he was a willing helper in the fight against crime, a pawn in a hideous game of real-life chess about to be sacrificed to win a deadly game, or a hostage on his way to his death. Sitting in the back of the BMW speeding effortlessly towards whatever awaited them, Callum thought about his brother Iain…what did he really know about him? Iain had never told him about his real job at MI6, but then why would he? Callum had shown no signs of being able to teletransfer until this week. Callum remembered the time three years earlier when Iain was at home for Easter that he had woken Callum at 2 am by bursting into his room and telling him he was late for school and would miss his bus. Callum had got up, still half asleep, got dressed and run to the bus stop with all his stuff for the week, with Iain hurrying him all the way "C'mon Cal, run or you'll miss it!" Callum had realised the April Fool's joke only when he was standing at the bus stop, alone, with the stars twinkling overhead and a dawning memory that he was on school Easter holidays. Iain had laughed for days and it was only now, sitting in the back of the BMW that Callum found himself smiling at the practical joke for the first time. Iain was his brother! He had known Iain all his life! Was Iain really driving him to his death? Perhaps it was time to tell Iain what he knew about Doctor Slack's plans. Then another memory surfaced. A memory of the look he'd seen on Iain's face whenever Callum was the centre of attention at family gatherings, when the TV had come back a couple of years ago to do the piece on the ten year anniversary of the 'Boy on the boat' story. Maybe he'd wait to see how this played out before he confided in Iain.

Just then, a voice came through what was clearly a radio system and Iain picked up a telephone handle which

Callum hadn't seen before. After a few minutes of sotto voce chatting Iain replaced the handle and looked up.

"It looks like you were right Callum. They have been spotted near Kilcreggan, where apparently Slack has rented a shoreside cottage a year or so ago. Now it could really be a holiday retreat, or…it was mighty handy that you took this way Callum …is there anything you might like to share wi us Callum?"

For the first time Callum thought he could hear a touch of menace in his adopted brother's voice.

"Just lucky I guess" he muttered and slid even further into the leather seats.

Callum took out his phone and worryingly the battery was down to 45% already. He updated Emma on the situation and was peeved that he didn't get an instant reply. The miles and the hours swept effortlessly past until at lunchtime they pulled into a roadside pub and stopped for a sandwich.

"The nearest government installation from Slack is the submarine base at Faslane, so I have arranged for my team to meet us there. We'll hole up and see where he leads us" was the report that Iain gave after he re-joined Karen and Callum in the pub that they had holed up in. Either Iain was telling the truth and was just playing the situation as it developed, or he had an ulterior motive for wanting to be at the submarine base.

"We will go straight there and await developments," said Iain.

They all got back in the BMW with Callum feeling an ever greater sense of impending doom.

Emma was right. Here was his brother Iain taking him right to Slack, although it had been him who had insisted on the route south that took them past Faslane. How did Karen fit in? Was she simply a policewoman on secondment to this operation…did the police even do that? What about the MoD authorities at Faslane? He knew that the MoD had blocked the police looking into Slack in too much detail but surely they couldn't want Slack to take possession of a nuclear warhead? If Slack needed Carl's teletransference abilities, then surely it meant that they were stealing the warhead without the knowledge of the MoD? Or maybe they just needed it to look like a robbery? This is just too complicated!

Who to trust and who not to? Emma, he could definitely trust Emma. Callum smiled.

As they rounded a corner, Callum could see the naval base at Faslane come in to view and he was seized with a panic. He took one look at the size of the installation, the soldiers guarding the gate, and decided he had to be on the outside. Somewhere where he could be safe and still transfer. Somewhere where he could hide but still sense his body if he needed to.

"Stop the car I'm going to be sick!"

Karen cast a quick look behind her and could see Callum's face, white as a sheet in the rear-view mirror and the BMW ground to a halt. Callum opened the door and leaned forward as if to be sick but instead he rolled out of the car, on to his feet and straight across the road, over the ditch with a leap and straight up the very steep hill between the tightly packed coniferous trees.

"Callum!"

Callum could hear Iain shouting after him as he ran straight up the hill. Iain may have been bigger, older, and stronger, but when it came to running straight up a very steep hill he was never going to be able to catch his little brother. At the start of the chase, Callum had barely 10 metres start. After 100 metres he was easily 25 metres in front and the gap was getting increasingly large. Iain inevitably gave up and walked disconsolately back down the hill to the car. After ten minutes or so from his vantage point high up on the hill overlooking the loch, Callum could see the BMW pull into the compound that marked the Faslane Naval Base.

From his vantage point, overlooking the base, Callum could see that breaking in to the base would be a remarkable achievement. The Loch itself was about a kilometre wide and was obviously very deep. From so high up Callum could see the anti-submarine nets strung across the loch further towards Loch Long, the Clyde and the open sea, and the three parallel fences with dogs patrolling the inner fences. The main entrance had two gates with only one open at any one time, with soldiers with machine guns inspecting every car that went in and out. It looked impregnable! There was no way any human was going to get in there. But that was the problem, and Callum knew it. There was not going to be any human required to get in there to do what Slack and Carl intended. There were three huge warehouses built over the water which, Callum presumed, was where the subs would come in and out for refurbishment and repairs when they weren't out in the oceans of the world providing Britain's nuclear deterrent against…who? Callum wasn't sure any more. He knew that it used to be Russia…but now?

Callum rang Emma and explained the situation. She had said that the links between the two thugs who had kidnapped her parents and Slack were getting clearer the more she was able to hack into the banks' computers. Callum felt very uneasy about the law breaking that was going on in cyberspace but felt reassured that at least he had Emma on the outside who knew where he was and what he was going to do. If it all went wrong she could at least talk to her contacts at MI6. Or she could hide her tracks and maybe keep herself and her parents safe. Emma also told him that Karen the policewoman was from a small town in Shropshire called Ludlow. She was 32, had done well at school (her father was a joiner and her mother was a primary school teacher). She had gone to University in London and got a first class honours degree in Psychology. After University, she had travelled for a year and then joined the Metropolitan Police where she was firearms trained and often worked on anti-terrorism projects. Her police files had a few commendations from MI6 so clearly, she had worked with them before. There was no connection to Slack, or LSD, or anything else they had learned.

Towards the end of the conversation Emma had asked him what he intended to do.

"Don't worry," he said, "I'll figure something out." He hadn't sounded convincing to either of them.

And what exactly was he going to do?

Callum wasn't sure, but each of the defences could be got past easily by an animal of one sort or another. He needed to figure out Slack and Carl's plan to get in, but then how would they get something as huge as a nuclear warhead out? He couldn't figure out how Slack and Carl were going to do it. The good news from his perspective was that he didn't need to figure it out. All he needed to do was stop it.

One thing he was sure of, and that was that the plan involved both land and water elements. The initial approach could come from anywhere, but Callum felt it likely that it would come by water. He was confident for three reasons. The first is that this was where security was weakest. To let a sub in to the heart of the base, you had to have a very big gate. The second was that you couldn't stop marine animals from swimming up and down next to the sub when it came in, and the third reason is that one of the tanks in the yacht held an otter…perfect for going from the sea to the land and, even if it was spotted it wouldn't be as obvious as a monkey or a golden eagle. Sure, golden eagles are as native to this part of Scotland as otters but they tend to be shyer and far less likely to turn up on a nuclear submarine base. Callum cast his mind back and tried to remember the creatures he had released as the monkey when he was on the yacht. Obviously, there was the monkey, the eagle, the otter, a snake, and a cockroach. Was there anything else that he hadn't seen?

The eagle could be used to get here, and the otter to get past the sea defences, but what had they in mind for the snake, the monkey and the cockroach? Perhaps they were just for Carl to practice on. Somehow Callum doubted it. Maybe Emma would figure it out. He flipped the phone open for the umpteenth time that day noticing the battery worryingly low at 22% and started a long text.

Throughout the afternoon there had been considerable activity on the base, but apart from the landing of a helicopter, which Callum assumed was the arrival of the 'team' that Iain had referred to, Callum had no idea of the significance of the activity. Neither had he any idea of how this 'burglary' would happen. He couldn't imagine a frontal assault being successful, so it had to be using Carl's skills and subterfuge. Assuming a vessel big enough to take a nuclear warhead away, it had to get in and out without being attacked and Callum had no idea at all as to how that could be achieved. So he waited and watched.

Chapter 15

Friday Afternoon Carl

"Doctor, are you sure that the effects of the drugs have worn off?" asked Carl.

"Yes, Carl, thank you for your concern but I would be grateful if you would concentrate on the task at hand. Are you sure that you have memorised tonight's codes?"

"Yes Doctor." Carl replied his voice cold and slightly bored.

"And are you certain that you can master the cockroach again?"

"Yes Doctor. I transferred three times this afternoon. That girl did us a favour. I discovered that a degree of necessity gives me the extra imperative I need to get into an insect. Their minds are so different to our own, it is a difficult one to master."

"And you have the required animals in place?"

"Yes Doctor. With the loss of our own eagle I had to go to the house in Oban and bring the eagle and monkey from there."

"Good, so we are all set?"

"Yes Doctor."

"Doctor?"

"Yes Carl?"

"When we retrieve the warhead, why will they not track us using the sub?"

"Carl, the MoD are not free-thinking. When they realise the loss, they will need instructions, orders from London. London will be afraid of the consequences of such a huge loss, so they will need to go to the very top for authority and that takes time, enough time for us to disappear. When we are clear of a possible pursuit, we contact the world authorities and let them know that we are a force to be reckoned with. They will give us anything we want…not to return the warhead, but to keep quiet. The world would panic, the stock market would crash, and we would plunge into a vicious recession if the world knew that its nuclear powers were not able to keep the nuclear warheads safe."

"Would they not come after us?" asked Carl.

"They would think about it of course. The British SAS or the American Navy Seals…even Mossad from the Israelis, but if we protect ourselves with automatic simultaneous web and TV broadcasts announcing the loss of the warhead we will be safe…like in the cold war between the Western Allies and the USSR (the Russians)…we would be relying on 'mutually assured destruction'. They could track and kill us, but then we could destroy confidence in the UK Government by releasing details of the warhead. The amount that 'UK Plc' would lose would be phenomenal. The mere £1 billion that we are demanding in ransom to remain silent about the warhead is a tiny amount to pay. After all, we are reasonable people, we don't want death and destruction...only money. After they have paid the money, they could then be blackmailed over the fact that they have paid the ransom money. So it would be naïve to think that they wouldn't know it was us...in fact I have a feeling that they already know we are planning something... and that they could come after us and kill us but with the knowledge we could flood the world's media with the truth about a nuclear warhead, we are untouchable! No, Carl, we will be untouchable, just like we are over the LSD operation. Never forget Carl, that knowledge is power and even apart from your undoubted talents, we are very powerful."

"It truly is a brilliant plan Doctor."

"It is," the Doctor agreed, "but not my greatest work... This is just a means to an end. Once we are untouchable and rich beyond reason, I will publish my results and you will be the proof. The proof that I am probably the greatest scientist since..." at this point Doctor Slack stopped, looked at Carl and said "well, ever really! The greatest scientist ever! I will have taken mankind beyond evolution into the realms of Gods. The Nobel prize will be mine and the recognition that I have long deserved."

"Now Carl...go and fly the area and see what there is to see. No doubt there will be additional security, but I doubt whether they will have changed the fundamentals of that security, so we can go ahead with our plans this evening. Ten thousand extra soldiers could not stop you. Carl, you are my magnificent creation!"

Carl took off from the deck on the trawler that was then two miles off the mouth of Gareloch. Far enough away to be beyond the exclusion zone around the base, but close enough for their plans and easily within the flight capability of the eagle and the swimming distance of the otter although it was getting close to its limit. He and the Doctor had gone through their plans meticulously again and again and while there was always the possibility of failure, he felt that he had minimised it as much as was humanly possible. Although the stealing of the nuclear warhead had been the Doctor's idea, it was he, Carl who had refined the plan and done the research that had unearthed the weakness in the security systems. Also, it was he who would actually steal the warhead, so it was he who had to ensure that the plan was still possible.

Carl opened the vast wingspan of the golden eagle, Britain's largest raptor and let the wind lift him off the deck, with mighty beats of his wings he rose in the cool evening air. While the eagle would not normally be this far out at sea, it had little fear, before the people came, there was nothing to fear for the great bird that ruled the tops of the highest peaks, soaring majestically in thermals. It was people who decimated the numbers of these beautiful creatures, blaming them for taking sheep. Luckily the laws had changed in the last 30 years and their numbers were slowly on the increase, so a golden eagle soaring above the sub base would be admired but not cause any undue alarm or activity.

Carl flew higher and higher and drifted until he was circling at over a kilometre straight up. His eyesight was such that he could make out all the detail he needed. He too saw the sub as it made its way into the Loch, he too saw the man looking up at him with binoculars and he too saw the owl circling like an idiot in the evening gloom. Carl knew instantly that this was no ordinary owl. No owl circled like that just looking. It had to be Callum his twin. As he thought about that, Carl considered his feelings towards his natural brother, to discover that he didn't have any, none at all...although that wasn't quite true...when he looked deeper inside himself he knew that the only feeling he did have was dislike. Callum was probably the only person who could stop them, and he was the only competition to himself. So if Callum died this evening, the Doctor would be disappointed but he would understand the threat that Callum posed to their plans.

Carl focussed the eagle's attention toward the owl and put his head down, his wings back and his talons forward. A hurtling missile of death. If Carl could strike quickly enough Callum wouldn't know what had hit him, wouldn't have time to snap back to his body, and would be dead instantly while still in the sky.

Chapter 16

Friday Afternoon Callum

Callum still didn't know exactly what the plan was to get into the base, and still had no idea as to how Slack and Carl would get the missile out but a text from Emma was beginning to make sense...

What can a cockroach do? What can an eagle do? What can a snake do? What can a monkey do? What can an otter do? E

Callum felt like Emma was setting him some sort of test which was pretty annoying but it wasn't a hard test...a cockroach can go anywhere, an eagle can fly and it is a big bird with big talons so it can carry...a monkey has fingers and thumbs and an otter can swim. All of this was obvious, but how did it all go together? Callum could clearly see the animals being used to get into the base but what then?

Callum had no idea how big a nuclear warhead was but surely it was too big for an eagle or a monkey to carry?

Whatever it was, Callum had to disrupt the plan and make a big fuss. A big fuss and the security would be tightened and then surely they couldn't break in (although with Carl's abilities Callum didn't really believe that), but more importantly if security was high enough then surely they couldn't break out with a missile...but Iain was in there, presumably making sure that security was as tight as possible...or completely useless. Still it wouldn't hurt to make a noise!

With that Callum let his mind search away from his body and very quickly found a gull flying around the loch. With a nauseating lurch that was nothing compared to how hard it had been just a few days earlier to teletransfer... odd how even the word that had been so new to him only a few days before now sat comfortably in his mind... Callum was in the gull and flying down towards one of the soldiers guarding the front gate.

The soldier was from Birmingham and as was his duty was standing with his legs apart and his M16 semi-automatic rifle held across his chest with the strap taking the weight on his left shoulder. His right hand was comfortably held around the grip with his finger resting lightly on the trigger as was normal when the base was in this heightened state of alert. The soldier had no idea why the base had gone to its highest state of readiness just after he had let the BMW in earlier in the day, but it didn't worry him. He was a soldier in the British Army and would do his duty whatever. What was worrying him however was a gull that was walking quietly and steadily towards him. It appeared quite fearless and really wasn't acting like a gull at all... as it got closer he swung a boot at it, but it just jumped, flapped its wing and flew straight for his right hand and pecked really hard at his trigger finger. The finger spasmed and the muscles contracted and inevitably the gun released 3 shots in rapid succession that had exactly the result that Callum wanted...sirens...running feet...everyone on an even more heightened state of alert. As Callum took off (he didn't want the gull punished), he felt a bit sorry for the soldier who would no doubt struggle to explain what had just happened.

Now the next stage of Callum's plan...to find out exactly what the Doctor's and Carl's plans really were. He turned the gull and flew straight out to sea, gaining in height all the time.

It was a gamble, Callum was gambling on the otter. The otter could swim, the otter could get away, on land, in rivers, in the sea. The otter could get away in the sea and it was this thought that drove Callum to fight his growing weariness and the pull from his own body. It was a jigsaw and the pieces were beginning to fit...Carl would need to get away and he would need to feel his body while he was teletransfering, so his body needed to be visible, exposed, but safe...and the otter could swim...it had to be a boat. The Doctor and Carl had already shown their familiarity and ease on the sea so Callum was looking for a boat...and there it was! Dipping and rising in the north Atlantic swells, a bottom dragging trawler with its nets deployed, and as he got closer he could see what looked like himself lying on the top of the bridge, same golden hair, same toned body, same mother and same father. Very different boy.

And then he knew, like a blinding flash in his head he knew how they would do it. He knew how they would get the nuclear warhead out. It was so simple, and so brilliant! He also knew what each of the animals were for, the animals that had led him to guess that the sea was key to his twin's plans, to the boat that would take the warhead, or more probably the whole missile.

Callum knew what Slack and Carl were going to do and he also knew that no normal security could stop them. It was down to him. Down to him to stop the most brilliant, audacious theft ever attempted.

Callum wheeled and flew back towards the base and his body, he would have been quicker just letting go and returning to his body leaving the gull out over the water where it would happily just carry on with its life, but the transfers were tiring him and flying tired the bird rather than Callum. This filled him with some sort of guilt. He hadn't considered it before but what right did he have to just occupy an animal and make it do his bidding? He remembered the rabbit that had died on his first transfer and wondered if that would have been the outcome if he hadn't been in it. Yes, almost certainly it would have died, but what about the other animals he had used? He thought about leaving Lottie out on the Craignure road, the headache he must have given the orca, the distress he'd caused the owl forcing it to fly out over the sea at night, and most tragically the monkey, shot to death by one of Slack's stooges. It wasn't right, but what else could he do?

It was 9.30 pm before it started to get dark and Callum was getting cold, tired, and hungry. He had been careful to keep out of sight of the air and possible flying twin brothers but that meant staying within the trees and that in turn meant an earlier nightfall and a more restricted view of the base. Callum was getting worried about his phone battery which was now at 14% following an exchange of texts in which Emma told him that she now had cast iron proof of the link between the kidnappers and the Doctor, and also some very incriminating evidence against the MoD with respect to the LSD manufacturer on Iona, Callum decided that he needed to get closer to the base, while leaving his body on the hilltop where he could sense it.

For the second time that day, Callum reached out with his mind and as he was hoping, found a short-eared owl just beginning to stir for the evening's hunt. The teletransfer was now accomplished with ease and he flew the bird down off the hilltop and over the base. As he expected, there was a lot of to-ing and fro-ing at the base. There was a clutch of buildings all surrounded by the sea or by the fencing that ran right down and into the sea, and the three large warehouses that looked as if they floated above the water, although Callum couldn't see if they floated or were on stilts in the water. Callum guessed they probably floated as he knew that the Loch was chosen for its depth, its inaccessibility from the east and its easy access to the North Atlantic where a sub could disappear from its enemies quickly.

As he circled he saw that the majority of the activity was centred around one of the warehouses…the one nearest the sea entrance to the loch and then he saw it. Under the crystal-clear waters of the Loch he could see it, the vast shape of the submarine coming into the docking station in the warehouse; huge, sleek, beautiful and ugly at the same time, hidden from the world carrying its deadly weapons of mass destruction, the Royal Navy nuclear submarine was coming in to dock.

Callum was entranced by the activity and continued to circle, watching as the huge weapon slid beneath the roofed warehouse. His reverie was broken, and his attention attracted by a dull glinting. Someone on the ground was watching him through binoculars that were reflecting the fading light from the west. With his incredible owl's night vision eyesight, he could see that it was Iain. Callum cursed his foolishness. If Iain could pick him out so easily then so could Doctor Slack and Carl. He tried to turn nonchalantly away from the base (if an owl can be nonchalant) and the turn saved his life. Travelling at nearly 100 miles an hour the shape of a golden eagle shot past him, but not before one of its talons ripped through his wing and he fell out of the sky. Tumbling, the owl inside terrified of its impending death.

CHAPTER 17

FRIDAY EVENING CARL

After dealing with Callum, Carl returned with the eagle to
the trawler and landed next to his body. By not transferring
he could save energy that he would need later. Two of the
Doctor's 'employees' were waiting for him with the monkey
which was sedated and had various items attached to its
body, the first looked a bit like a matchbox, the second
was obviously a gas mask already securely fastened to
the monkey's face and the third looked like a hypodermic
strapped to the arm.

Carl stuck his right talon towards the man who strapped
what looked remarkably like a firework to his leg.

Carl was surprised that the Doctor wasn't on the
bridge to see him off but engrossed as he was in the task
at hand he merely hopped to the monkey, grabbed it by

the arms and opened his huge wings for the second time that evening. The eagle was getting tired and didn't want to do what he was asking of it. Carl opened its mind and stimulated the pain centre in a brutal display of power. The eagle complied and took off towards the east and the base 2 miles away. Even with its burden, it completed the flight quickly and silently. In what was now a black and overcast night no one saw the eagle's flight, and even if they had they wouldn't have believed what they had seen.

"Och Angus, an eagle wi a monkey ye say? Have ye no been a little free with the wee dram?"

Carl didn't waste any time…he knew exactly where he was going and he landed right in the middle of the roof of the warehouse where earlier in the evening he had seen the sub dock. In the middle of the roof was a small structure about knee height that looked remarkably like a mushroom. This was the air intake for the air conditioning units that right now were pumping cooled, clean, dry air throughout the building, into the submarine, down into the bridge of the sub, and into the missile deployment room. The room where, in the event of nuclear war, the two most senior officers would read their orders, and insert their two keys, without which, the warhead could not be fired.

The air conditioning units for a nuclear submarine base are surprisingly not that much different to those which adorn the sides of houses in hot countries, and just like them these air conditioning units were designed to cool and remove moisture. They weren't designed to remove toxic nerve agents. So when Carl pecked at the top of the firework and gas started to stream out of the tube strapped to his leg it was sucked into the air conditioning and in 2 minutes everyone in the building and in the sub was asleep. Not a nice restful sleep but a drug induced sleep that would leave them with a brutal headache when they awoke in about 12 hours time, long after Carl had left and way too late to stop this theft.

Carl had been in his eagle for about 40 minutes, he was aware that time was ticking by so he wasted no time in picking up the monkey and dropping down to ground level in a dark unlit corner. He pecked the button next to the syringe which when released, slid into the monkey's arm and immediately Carl took off…he didn't want a disorientated eagle flapping about drawing attention from the patrols that regularly swept the grounds of the base. While he was taking off, he let his mind search for that of the monkey and as it started to wake from its drug induced slumber he transferred into it, leaving the eagle to let out a single cry and continue up into the mountains to the north of the Loch and to freedom.

Carl waited a few minutes for the monkey's body to respond to his demands. The monkey was very frightened but with a force of will Carl made it run to the door to the main warehouse. The buttons were just out of the monkey's reach but by repeatedly jumping and pushing buttons it was able to input the door code and the door slid soundlessly open. The monkey inside was screaming to remove the mask but Carl effortlessly kept it under control. They passed many bodies on their way to heart of the sub…six security doors, a lift, and couple of ladders gave Carl no trouble and then he was in the missile launch centre. At last he was nearly there!

The monkey jumped to the top of the missile control centre to find a computer console surrounded by buttons and lights…and the two key slots, keys without which the missiles couldn't be armed or launched.

The monkey's fingers flew over the glowing screen, Carl had practiced this a hundred times back on the yacht, before his twin had destroyed it…still he was dead now so no more interference and competition from him. Carl examined his own feelings about that and discovered he had none…the brat had meddled too much and had got what was coming to him.

It had amazed Carl how easily people were bribed to reveal the codes and passwords that could get him into the sub-base warehouse and even into the control room and the missile launch control program. Still he supposed that they consoled themselves in the knowledge that without the two keys that were presumably either around the necks of the officers or securely locked away from each other, anything they sold was useless. Still Carl didn't care. This had to be a one-man operation…one boy operation, so the keys were always out of the question.

As his fingers flew, setting the launch sequence going, selecting coordinates and most importantly disarming the warhead, Carl prepared himself for his most difficult teletransfer yet that evening.

CHAPTER 18

FRIDAY NIGHT

Callum could feel the owl start to shut down. The pain in its wing and the shock of having been hit by the eagle was too much for its small bird brain and it was shutting down, to fall out of the sky and hit the ground inside the fences of the base in a fall that would certainly be fatal. Callum prepared to teletransfer out of the owl and back to his body where he would be safe, but he didn't want to leave the bird to its fate. His human brain lying back on the hilltop knew that the damage to the wing wasn't too bad and that maybe the owl could fly out of this if only he could persuade it to. Callum reached deep into the owl's senses. He could feel the pain in the wing and the total despair in the owl's tiny brain and he took them away, he didn't know how, just like he didn't know how he could teletransfer at all, but he did.

He took them on himself, he took the pain and he took the despair and urged the owl to open its wings and fly.

It was a close-run thing but the owl opened its wings and flew, more glided, over the fence and across the road into the first trees at the bottom of the hill. I'm sorry, he thought to the owl, if I make it I will come back and help you. With that he snapped back to his body, feeling more tired than he could believe possible, reminding him of his brush with the orca, and that had turned out OK... He was desperately hungry and needed to sleep to recharge, but he couldn't afford to. Carl had been reconnoitring the base and now that he thought Callum was dead he would be back soon enough, and Callum had to stop him.

So, in the end, Carl hadn't got into the warehouse completely unobserved. An otter, that had been playing near the water had swum along the edge of the base lying on its back eating a shellfish... a perfectly normal thing for an otter to do, but not so late in the evening and not looking straight up the whole time. As soon as it saw the eagle with its unlikely load alight on the roof it scampered out of the water and watched the eagle take off and drop the monkey on the floor outside the building. The eagle took off, and Callum was tempted to use the otter to attack the monkey there and then, but he wasn't sure of the outcome. Callum could feel the otter inside desperate to run back to the water where it would feel safe, so Callum let it, but not before he had poked its nose inside the building and seen the bodies slumped where they had fallen. Back outside, he let the otter go and snapped back to his body. Carl was clearly inside and the eagle had done its job. Callum had no idea whether the bodies were dead or merely drugged but he didn't want to go in to find out. He reached for his phone… his one link to the outside … the battery was at 3%… and texted Emma.

Guards asleep or dead. Get help now.

Just as he hit send, the phone finally died, its battery exhausted.

Did it go? Is help coming?

There was just one chance to stop Carl now. Although Callum didn't know how Carl was going to do it he knew that there would be at least one more transfer for Carl tonight and when he did it, he Callum would be ready. One more transfer into a tiny unthinking insect that was commonly thought to be one of the only things that could survive a nuclear holocaust… now that's irony, thought Callum as he let his mind reach out to find the scared mind of a small primate somewhere in the depths of the submarine. Callum was gutted he was wrong about the otter and the snake but he was certain the cockroach was to be key to this audacious robbery.

The system was armed, the timer initiated, the only things missing were the two keys. Carl knew that the timers would run down to zero and then the microprocessor controller circuitry would switch to old-fashioned analogue circuitry, deemed by the MoD to be more reliable in the last few seconds before the final relay closed triggering the launch. Two keys were all it would take now…or one short circuit. One place deep in the consul where if something were to short out, the circuits would fire the missile with or without the two keys. The single point of weakness in the whole procedure.

Carl transferred out of the monkey and into the cockroach but only after the monkey had carefully emptied the contents of the box tied to its arm into the access panel on the console. 67 minutes had passed since Carl had first transferred into the eagle, but that wasn't the time constraint. He had only 2 minutes as the electronic counters timed down to get into position and so he concentrated with all his might and set the cockroach scurrying into one of the key holes and the heart of the electronic maze. As he scurried he could feel vibrations and see changes in… colour? The cockroach senses were so alien to those of a human he was struggling to interpret what the cockroach was experiencing. Of course!…it dawned on him…the inside of the sub's missile launch room was being flooded with sirens and warnings about the impending launch with the inevitable countdown and that was what the cockroach was sensing.

It amused him that there was no one there awake to hear them…there was always the monkey, but it would have ripped its mask off by now and would be as drugged as the people.

Carl was concentrating so hard on the cockroach, that he didn't notice that when he released the monkey it didn't do the monkey things that it usually did when he released it…ripping its mask off and running to the corner and rocking…instead it went to look at the console and the display.

Callum was exhausted. He wasn't as used to transferring as Carl and had done it too often over the last few days. He could hardly raise the strength to feel out with his mind. With a herculean effort he had felt for the monkey and instantly knew that Carl was there, so he backed off and waited, as soon as he felt Carl leave he teletransfered straight into the monkey. Just in time he stopped the monkey ripping its mask off. The monkey's senses were overwhelmed with the noise of a countdown and the brightness of a red flashing light right above the console but just like humans the monkey had evolved to spot movement and Callum was just in time to see the cockroach scurry into the key slot.

This was just what Callum had concluded earlier in the day. The plan was simple. Fire the missile to get it out of the base and pick it up with the ground nets of the trawler and then haul it up and take it out to sea and hide it and retrieve it later when the fuss had died down.

What Callum didn't know was exactly what the cockroach was supposed to do. Anyway, it didn't matter now. All he had to do was find the abort button, and with a monkey's opposable thumbs it should be easy enough! Callum was filled with confidence as he used the monkey's almost human eyes to scan the console in front of him.

"T minus 94 seconds"

"T minus 93 seconds"

"T minus 92 seconds"

"T minus 91 seconds"

All Callum could hear was the awful countdown! How was he supposed to concentrate! This thing looked like the pictures he'd seen of the inside of aircraft cockpits… the array of dials and knobs and displays was terrifying.

"T minus 43 seconds"

Agggghhhh shut up! There must be an abort somewhere... surely it would be a big red button... think!

Callum looked at the console again...buttons, displays, key holes...that was it! Key holes! Two keys needed to actually fire the missile...there didn't need to be an abort button! All you had to do was take out a key! But there aren't any keys.

"T minus 18 seconds"

So that was what the cockroach was for. It was inside the console and somehow meant that there was no need for a key.

Callum felt a sense of despair as he realised that all was lost. There was nothing he could do. Carl and Doctor Slack had won. They were going to launch a nuclear missile from a British submarine whilst in its base. They were going to steal it! He remembered the pictures he'd seen of the aftermath of Hiroshima and Nagasaki, the only two times in human history that nuclear weapons had been deliberately used against humans. He couldn't begin to wrap his head around what a disaster this would be... unless.

The cockroach was a simple creature and Carl had no difficulty controlling its movement. The difficulty was knowing where he was inside the console. He knew that he had to be in place as the countdown got to 0. The cockroach would then be the conduit for the electricity to fire across two contacts. As soon as that electricity flowed the missile would launch and there would be nothing that could stop it. It had been imperative to get to the sub just after it arrived back from patrol or the missiles wouldn't be live, and still onboard but it took a day to remove them and the sub had only been back a few hours.

The cockroach would be fried by the electricity flowing through its body, but he was confident that he could snap back to his body as the cockroach sacrificed its life to complete the perfect crime.

There. He had felt the two large connectors just below the keyholes. Now all he had to do was wait and be very very quick to get out of this body as it fried!

Callum had to try. He was so tired he almost gave up but the last thing he had heard from his father "Do the reet thing," galvanised him to one last gargantuan effort.

Callum wasn't a coward. He'd never run from a fight at school but he did try his best to diffuse them. He kept away from the bigger bullies, he used his smile and his quick tongue to talk people out of fights and he was so good at it that he had only ever had one fight...which he lost. It was more his pride than his body that had been wounded, but he was scared now. Scared of what he might encounter, scared of his twin and scared of dying. He was 12 years old. He didn't want to die.

So it was with fear and exhaustion that he reached out with his mind and found the cockroach. It was a strange feeling to reach out to an animal that already had a passenger. He could sense it.

He knew he had no choice but to do this. He pushed and suddenly he was in... inside the mind of a cockroach already occupied by his twin brother.

"You! I thought you were dead!" Carl's outrage was palpable to both of them. His shock flooded through the cockroach's tiny mind and could be felt by both of them.

"It would take more than you in an eagle to kill me!"

"I can see what you are doing, and you cannot beat me in here! This cockroach is not moving no matter how hard you try to make it. We are stealing this missile and there is nothing you can do to stop us!"

Callum knew that Carl was right. He felt the superior power that Carl had over the cockroach. He tried to force the cockroach to run...nothing. He opened the cockroach's mind but there wasn't enough there to work with. Callum knew that there really wasn't anything he could do, that Carl had won. He felt the despair of the young rabbit he had dived on as a buzzard... despair and helplessness.

"T minus 1 second"

"LAUNCH"

Ha ha ha! The fool! Did he really think he could challenge me? His attempts to control the cockroach are pathetic. He doesn't have the power that I do! Still it is impressive that he could get into the 'roach at all after such a short time. It is very strange sharing a creature with another teletransferrer. There are probably only two of us left in the world who can do this. Me and my twin brother. My twin brother. A creature I shared a mother and father with. My only living family. And now he is going to die. He is going to die...unless I...why would I? He is exhausted, beaten, and waiting for death. A death that is coming to him NOW.

Carl snapped back to his body just as 15V arced along

the cockroach's body completing the electrical circuit that started the chain reaction of opening the sub missile hatch and igniting the fuel of the cruise missile. The cockroach died instantly as the missile started to rise into the air, seemingly slowly at first but with increasing speed and momentum, bursting through the roof of the floating warehouse as if it wasn't there and adopting a very shallow arc, heading west, over the end of the loch and streaking out over the Irish Sea.

Chapter 19

Saturday Lunchtime

"Hi Cal, ye med it then ya wee hero!"

As Callum opened his eyes he could see his brother Iain sitting on his bed... his hospital bed.

"Where am I?"

"Glasgee Royal Infirmary,"

"What time is it?"

"2 o'clock on Saturday afternoon."

"Did it launch?"

"Aye, and they picked it up in the nets in the trawler they had ready off the coast of Donegal. They've picked it up, moved it and dropped it. We're looking, but without coordinates, it will be almost impossible to find. Also, we've been warned not to look, or Slack will release his press releases and video all over the world at the same time.

That's what he was doing in the trawler at the mouth of the loch. Filming the launch and simultaneously uploading it to a cloud-based server. He's got us Cal. If we tek him in or look for the warhead, he will tell the world that we lost one and that would be a disaster. He and Carl have won for now.

Cal, later I'll have to ask you for two statements. One for me…the truth, the whole truth of what happened, and then one for Karen. A statement that says that you fell asleep on the top of the hill and then felt ill. A statement that says that you lost your phone and you have nae idea what those messages were on it. Can you do that for me Cal?"

Callum just looked at his brother.

"And Cal, I'm sorry"

"Fer what?"

"Fer not telling you everything. Fer not telling you that you aren't my only assignment, Emma told me that you thought I could have been one of the bad guys. You are part of my assignment. My only assignment. I have been looking into the LSD trafficking operation, Slack, the folk in the MoD that have been funding and shielding him, and into the claims of the servicemen who were experimented on in the 90s. We believe them Cal, and the government will be settling their claims and looking after them. The MoD treated them terribly. Your friend Emma is amazing. The things she can do and the places she can go online. With the info she's given me, we will be making significant arrests, of the gang running the LSD operation and also a few highly placed folk in the MoD. It's a good job she's 12 or I would have to arrest her! As it is, we have a place waiting for her as soon as she is ready for it."

"So who do ye really work for then?"

"Like I said I work for MI6 on secondment from the Polis but I'm no supposed to ever admit that, so I havnae. Within MI6 there is a very special, very small team of people who look into things that no one else would ever believe. On teletransference, there is only two of us. Me and my boss, and she is very very high up…I get a lot of authority from her."

"Who is she?"

"That's something I cannae tell you…ever."

Callum felt exhausted and fell back on his pillow his mind racing. Maybe he'd been foolish not trusting Iain.

"Are ma and pa here?"

"Aye Cal, I couldnae stop them from coming."

Callum sighed and mentally prepared himself for the onslaught of love and attention and recriminations that would bustle in in the form of Mrs McBride and the slightly less animated form of Mr McBride.

"Cal, I can read yer mind!" said Iain laughing.

"I've arranged for them to get lost in here…it's a big place, so you've got mebe 10 minutes… Shall I show her in?"

Iain stood up, ruffled Callum's hair and went to the door. He opened it and waved. Emma came in and stood next to the bed.

"You didn't die then?" she asked matter of factly.

Callum wasn't sure what he expected…but it wasn't this…in his mind they had been through a massive ordeal together and he expected…he expected…well he had no idea, but this cold question wasn't it.

He sighed internally and took a deep mental breath. He really didn't want to fall out with Emma and every time he'd reacted to something she'd said, it had gone badly so he was determined to stay friendly.

"No… I nearly died though. He saved me."

"What do you mean he saved you? Who saved you?"

"Carl. When he killed the cockroach using it to conduct electricity he could have left me there to die with it, but he didn't, he kicked me out of the teletransfer. I'm not sure how to explain it. He could have done it at any time. He is much better at it than I am and he could have kicked me out of the cockroach at any time but he didn't, he left me there until the very last second and then he kicked me out…as he left himself. He saved me. He didn't have to, but he did."

"Are you sure he did it on purpose?"

"Aye. Certain, and he'd tried to kill me earlier when I was in an owl. Emma, why did he save me?"

Emma just stood looking at Callum. After a little while she said "The police have taken our phone's and my computer. I knew they would so mine is clean and I cleared out your email as well. Iain found you after I got your text and contacted the people from MI6 who were nice to me. There was a lady before, when no one believed that I could have done what I did she contacted my family and spoke to me. Anyway, when I got your last text…which was very misleading by the way you said they were going to launch and it took me a minute to work out what you meant. I thought you meant launch as in a boat…you could have been clearer…"

Callum could have jumped out of his bed, if he hadn't still felt so tired, and thumped Emma for being so ANNOYING, he bit his lip and waited to hear the rest.

"…I contacted her and told her that there was a robbery of a nuclear missile going on right then in Faslane and she believed me! She just asked if you were on site. I told her that you were on top of the hill overlooking the site and she contacted Iain and made him go and find you immediately. It was a good job that she did because apparently you were nearly dead when you arrived here with a whole load of soldiers and other people…oh and a monkey. I think the monkey was OK, they took it away to a zoo and all the soldiers woke up after a while. They were told that there had been a refrigerant gas leak but that's rubbish because…"

"Enough!" Exclaimed Callum. "You can give me all the details later but now we need to go, will you help?"

"Of course."

"Will you go and get Iain and tell him that we need a car and a phone, and we need to get to Faslane as soon as we can? Tell him that I need this favour and then after that I will do anything he wants, I'll even go willingly with Ma but I need this and I need it now!"

It took a bit of persuading for Iain to agree to all of Callum's demands, but he could see that Callum wasn't for being persuaded otherwise. He could see that Callum would have tried to use his power to get there anyway so in the end he made a call and the car arrived. Callum was helped outside by his brother with Emma keeping a look out for Mrs McBride as neither brother wanted to run into her right now.

They got into the same car that only the day before had taken Callum to Faslane and Iain drove it himself, blue lights flashing all the way to Faslane. He laughed when he overheard the call Callum made on the way but didn't slow down at all.

On the way, Emma updated Cal on all the evidence she'd handed over to Iain. It did sound like there were two generals in the MoD who wouldn't see out their careers in the armed forces but in a cell guarded by those same armed forces. Whilst they were driving, Iain was on his radio and phone coordinating the rounding up of the LSD distribution from Iona all the way to the south of Italy and they heard live over the radio the storming of the 'religious community' on Iona and the discovery of a highly sophisticated laboratory.

They pulled up outside the Faslane Naval Base and pulled in to the side of the road just behind an RSPB van.

A young woman came bustling up to the rear window of the Jaguar and Callum wound down the window.

"Hi hun, was it yourself that called?" She looked a bit awed that the blue lights were still flashing, and that Callum clearly had his own driver. Iain just faced the front trying not to smirk.

"It was, there is an injured short eared owl in there, he said pointing to the first clump of trees maybe 10 metres off the side of the road."

"How do you know?"

"It was attacked by a golden eagle, I saw it"

The RSPB officer looked incredulously at Callum.

"Pleaaaase, go and look!"

She looked as if Callum were crazy.

"I'll never find her in there! Injured owls remain totally silent and I could search for weeks!"

"Please just try?"

She turned and started to walk into the woods turning and calling "Will you come and help?"

"I don't want to scare it."

She looked as if the whole lot of them were crazy.

Sharon was a sensible person, she had joined the RSPB 5 years ago because she wanted to help birds, to protect them and their environment, and most of all to look after and nurse injured birds. This was the weirdest call out ever. The kid was clearly crazy! The chances of finding an injured owl in here were zero! Still, she was prepared to try. It didn't matter if she ended up looking stupid if there was any chance she could find a suffering short eared owl. As she pushed on through the undergrowth she heard a noise…a bird call…wasn't that the call of a short eared owl? She turned towards it and to her absolute amazement saw an owl hopping towards her holding its damaged wing carefully by its side. She was used to netting wild birds and she already had her gloves on to protect her against the sharp talons and the nipping beak. She stood in amazement as the owl got closer and closer and hopped on to her hand as if it had been trained to do just that. She lifted her arm to give it a safe perch and walked out of the wood towards her van. As she did so, she looked back at the Jaguar police car, the blonde kid in the back looked like he was asleep. She opened the back of the van and opened a cage to put the owl in. It would be nursed back to health and then released in a couple of weeks into the same place, as good as new. Having made sure the owl was safe she turned to go back to the Police Jag, she had some questions that needed answering but as she did so the Jaguar turned in the road and roared away back towards Glasgow.

"Iain."

"Yes Cal?"

"Do we have to go back to Glasgow?"

"Why, where do you want to go?"

"Donegal. I can find that missile, even if you can't."

"I was hoping you might say that."

**The End
(For now)**

Visit www.callummcbride.co.uk